HeartBound

Layout by Brie Ehret Barron
Cover art © 2007 Brie Ehret Barron
Proofread by David MacHamer, Kelly Xuan Hay
Biography Photo © 2009 Bryon DeVore

Theohumanity©, Enheartenment©, & EBE©
are registered servicemarks of DS Barron

Printed by Outskirts Press, Inc.
http://www.outskirtspress.com

ISBN: 978-1-4327-6690-0
Library of Congress Control Number: 2010941771

Outskirts Press and the "OP" logo are trademarks belonging to Outskirts Press, Inc.

Printed in the United States of America

HeartBound

Daniel Stacy Barron

Outskirts Press, Inc.
Denver, Colorado

Also by DS Barron

Enheartenment
A full introduction to the paradigm of Theohumanity

There's no such thing as a negative emotion
The philosophical premises of Emotional Body Enlightenment
(EBE) dharma

Him
A disillusioned psychologist encounters a decidedly non-traditional
Jesus in His current incarnation at a cantina in Mexico

Gnospel
A new version of Genesis and the life and teachings of Jesus seen
through a new version of his human divinity

Contents

Dina

"Honey, who are you talking to?" Joyce called out to her 6 year-old daughter Dina, who was chatting melodically in the backyard, hearing her through the open window over the kitchen sink.

Dina had always been precocious. Joyce remembered when she was newborn and how hard it was from the beginning to get Dina to focus on what was right in front of her. She was born with eyes wide open and always seemed to be looking through people's faces to what was behind or above them. She started talking at two, but almost always to empty space, with pauses that made it seem like she was listening while an invisible speaker was responding.

Joyce and her husband Clay had been worrying how to get her ready for school that started in a few months, because Dina simply had never had any interest in basic social connections with other children or to focus on reading and numbering. She only politely tolerated adults, with a measured centeredness that wasn't cold, but certainly not warmly engaging. That response would change if you watched her from a short distance as she played alone, where she shined with the same warm glow as a fireplace, drawing you to her. But as you got close, that glow would fade, and her penetrating eyes would force you to step back.

"The light, mommy."

Joyce sighed as she pulled her hands out of the dishwater. Here we go again, she thought, shaking her head. It had been almost a month since Dina had had one of her conversations with nothing, and she and Clay had been crossing their fingers that maybe the phase had finally begun to pass once and for all.

As she walked out the back door she saw Dina sitting serenely in far corner of the yard, her chin raised and her face staring directly up into the foliage at the edge of the property. As her mother approached, she did not change her focus to acknowledge her mother's arrival.

Sitting down next to her cross-legged, Joyce said, "Who, honey?"

"The light, mommy .... ssshhh! I want to hear."

Joyce obeyed, wondering how she would approach Clay about needing to bring her back to Dr. Carmella again. Perfect, she thought: right when we need the money for the new roof, new gutters, and repairs to the fence.

"But what do I do then?" Dina asked her invisible cohort. As her voice trailed off, Dina tilted her head to the left as if straining to hear the answer.

"Dina, don't you think .... ."

"Mommy, ssshh! I can't hardly hear."

"Alright, but it's almost time for lunch."

Dina nodded absently, absorbed even more deeply, as if that were possible. Then she smiled and relaxed her face and said, "Okay. Thank you. Bye-bye."

Then she turned to her mother. "I'm hungry."

"Sure, bab .... but can you explain to mommy what you mean when you say you're talking to the light? You know we talked about you not looking straight into the sun."

Dina shook her head. "Soli the sun doesn't talk, mommy: he's too busy making sure everything grows right and worrying that all the flowers have enough shade. It's Miranda moon that talks, and she never wants to stop, like she's been waiting all day and she doesn't even take a breath between all the words. And right now I was talking to Lala the light who plays and swims all around the yard."

"I don't understand, Dina."

Dina's big eyes just looked up at Joyce with that same familiar helplessness, and Joyce knew her daughter was again struggling to share her experience with a world that simply did not know what she was talking about. But this was new: this was the first time Dina talked about speaking to Lala the light. Usually it was to Soli the sun, Terri the tree, Wando the wind, Miranda the moon, or Stellu the sky. But Soli, Terri, Wando, and Stellu always insisted they weren't the sun, trees, wind, or sky, that those were just word-names people made up.

Occasionally, she would also talk to their cat, whom Clay had named Jake. But at age two Dina had renamed him Zeebo, which she said the cat had said was his real name. Zeebo would always wind up rolling on his back when she spoke to him just wanting his belly rubbed, which he never did with anyone else ever. This had all started as soon as she began to talk, having conversations with voices and things and not people unless a person initiated it, and then only because she'd been told to respond.

"When Lala the light touches the leaves and the grass it makes a noise like someone whispering, and in between I can hear the words."

"And what did the light say?" Joyce asked. Dr. Carmella had told her to take her daughter's reality at face value so that once having joined her on the shore of her world, she could then lead Dina back to the ground of this one.

"She said that it would be hard for me to remember that everything talks, because the grown-ups forget and say that only people talk and that light and cats and trees can't."

Joyce frowned.

Dr. Carmella had warned that if Dina's voices began to speak in context instead of content, that is, having perspective about the conversations rather than just the words themselves and what they meant, then they had a different problem that would be much harder to solve. She had said that if that happened, it meant Dina would be starting to hold on more tightly and defensively to her private reality against the grain of how they had been trying to help her gradually let go of it.

Despite Clay's agreement with Dr. Carmella in that way, Joyce had been adamant about not wanting to make Dina feel wrong in having her fantasies. But since Dina stubbornly showed no proactive interest at all in people, other children, school, or being willing to stop talking to invisible speakers, Joyce had begun to see that she might have to acquiesce to some degree in that area. All the tests indicated that Dina wasn't autistic or impaired by any measure: in fact, she seemed to be just a hugely intelligent and hugely sensitive little girl with a strong proclivity to have conversations with empty air.

"So the light only has a voice when it touches other things?"

"Yes. Mommy. When it moves through the air it just sings without words. Only when it bumps into things does it get words."

"Does it talk when it bumps into the house and the car?"

"No. Just when it bumps into alive things."

"What about when it bumps into people?" Joyce continued.

Dina pouted and shook her head saying, "It just gets sad when it bumps into people because it says they never notice it because they live inside their heads too much."

"But it talks to you, and you're a people."

Dina was still for a long moment looking perplexed. Finally she said, "I'm .... a *people?*"

The look on her daughter's face shook Joyce to the core, but she was quick to catch herself so it didn't show. My God, my little girl actually doesn't know she's a person? What does that mean? "Of course, honey. When you look in the mirror, don't you see that you look like other kids and mommy and daddy and grandma and Brian and Laurie next door?"

Dina considered this for a moment and then began to cry, big wet tears rolling silently down her cherubic face. Joyce didn't know how to react, but she felt her daughter's sorrow in that moment and was completely paralyzed by the depth of it. My God, she thought. My child is so sad!

She struggled to recoup and said, "Dina, baby, what's wrong?"

"Mommy, how can I be a people if the light talks to me and I can hear it but no other peoples do?"

"Well, like Dr. Carmella said, what you hear is just inside your head and it will go away soon and then you won't feel so different than other kids."

"No!" Dina replied fiercely. "It's not inside my head, it's outside my head! I don't live inside my head like everyone else! I live inside my chest and go around in the inside of everything! And if I'm really a people, then that means I have to forget about talking with Lala and Wando and Miranda." She stood and stamped her feet. "I don't wanna forget! I don't wanna be a people! I wanna be a Dina forever and never ever be a people!"

"But Dina, mommy and daddy are people and we .... ."

".... never talk to anyone but other people!" she interrupted defiantly, completing her mother's sentence. "I don't wanna talk to people who only talk to other people, because then I might catch their kind of sick and I would forget everything too!"

This was new, Joyce thought. Everyone else is sick but she is not? Clay will go ballistic. "Dina, do you think people all have some kind of sickness that makes them not able to talk with everything like you?" she asked.

"Yes! Miranda Moon says that when people grow up they forget they are not people, and then think they have to live inside their heads to stay being people. That makes them sick with grown-up germs, and then the grown-ups make the children get sick with it too."

"But remember when Dr. Carmella said that .... ."

".... and I don't want to talk to that doctor any more because she thinks she's an extra smarty pants because she only talks to people like that's good and that I don't means I'm bad!"

Then she ran into the house, leaving Joyce in that same familiar space of helpless frustration. How can I get my daughter to come down to earth? There has to be a way. Clay will be livid hearing it has gone to another level now. How am I going to explain this new twist to him without him throwing up his hands and getting loud again?

This kind of thing was fine when she was younger, but it seemed like Dina just didn't want to grow up out of her childhood magical phase. She and Clay had gone to counseling but the therapist said there was nothing to indicate any aspect in their household or in their relationship that affected why Dina heard voices or her militant refusal to give them up, which of course gave Clay his 'I told you so.'

Maybe Clay was right. Maybe it was time to draw some boundaries and forbid her talking to empty space, and start giving her consequences if she did. What else could they do? Throwing more money at shrinks didn't seem to help. Yes. That's what we have to do.

If we love her, we have to start forbidding her to have these fantasies any longer. If we love her, we have to help her live in the real world. If we love her, we have to punish her for disobeying us.

I guess I was just trying to protect my daughter, and its time to do it Clay's and Dr. Carmella's way, she sighed to herself. I guess we'll have to go with the medication Dr. Carmella talked about, and see where to go from there. Then she got up and walked toward the house, thinking about how Dina had said she lived outside of herself and inside and around everything else. Why did that sound familiar? When I was young, didn't I .... ?

Kids, she thought, shaking her head hard to clear the thought. What can you do?

Dream

Sorrow without spite
must be what a flower feels
as it withers with the same sweetness
that it shouted its birth of bloom

I think
I could feel sorrow
that way

But without the heartsong
called out by a season of love
alive in a shared garden of green and purple
I can not go so gracefully into that good night
with so many seeds unopened
into the light of another's dawn of stars

So as dusk comes to a blameless world
that has always been color-blind
to the rainbows sparkling in my tears
so also will my pain wither
as yeast to bread of new heart-life
that may help feed others hungry
who come to God's table
in that rarely shared
feast
of
dream

Raymond

My name is Raymond, and you're probably not going to believe what I am about to tell you.

The nice thing about talking about it to a blank computer page in a word-processing document is that as a younger person, it avoids the face-to-face response by an adult when they find out you want to be a writer when you grow up. In my family, becoming a writer was considered somewhere between being a nightclub singer and a mafia hit-man. Actually, come to think of it, being a mafia hit-man would have gotten me a lot of positive attention in my particular family. But in most households, the only thing worse than a son who wants to be a writer is a daughter who wants to marry one.

I actually wanted to be an inventor even more than a writer. By the time most guys my age were trying to talk a girl into what the nuns were trying to talk them out of, I had invented a back-scratcher that was a fork attached to a pulley and foot pedal, and an automatic toilet paper dispenser. But since the use of the latter involves a lot of personal preference, my father drew the line on it. Add to those was something I called the Everything Machine. It whirred and beeped and had colored lights blinking on and off. I never did figure out what it actually was supposed to do, but it was beautiful!

I finished high school a year early and went to the state university in a small town on the other side of the county, and since my family never had much money, I had to find someone who would offer room and board in exchange for some chores around their place. Pretty much right away I found Quentin and Margo Blome, an elderly couple living in an old house that had a room above their garage their son used to live in. Seems like the son had succeeded with a girl where the nuns hadn't, gotten her pregnant, and had moved in with his girl-friend's parents to await the blessed event.

Quentin was the town's optometrist and ran its only optical lab. He'd been at it for over thirty years and loved the idea that something he made with his hands that compensated for someone's eyeballs having the nerve to be too long or too short or off-center for their owner. I quickly fell into a routine with Quentin's wife Margo cooking breakfast, Quentin dropping me off at school on his way to work, and walking back home after school for dinner and an occasional game of chess with Quent before books and bed.

The doc had a sort of a workshop rigged up in his basement where he spent most evenings to escape from Margo. She never went down there, and I was smart enough not to poke my nose into where it wasn't invited. If all he did was sit down there and look at porn on his computer that made sense to me, since just about anything was better than having to hear Margo carping endlessly about how Quentin had promised her to provide for her in the manner she had been accustomed. Her father had been the town M.D. and she could never understand why an O.D. didn't make as much money as an M.D. (quote: 'They're both something-D's aren't they?' unquote.)

But I liked school and the doc took over as honorary uncle. He and I shared a common love for things that did what they were designed to do and a common disdain for the nightly sermon delivered by her highness. All in all, my world was nothing to complain about.

One evening we blew a fuse with Margo vacuuming, me watching TV and Quent running something in the basement. Quent called up the stairs for me to bring down a new one, his house still running with those old screw-in type fuses and not the ones that flip before they burn out. As I inched my way down the stairs in the dark, the doc grabbed my wrist and led me to the fusebox. When the lights came on I found myself standing in a room that ran the full length of the house, with a room down at the far end with a door slightly ajar. An unusual light glowed out of the opening, too bright to be from a lamp.

"Ever wonder what I do down here, Ray?" Quentin asked.

"Sure. But I didn't want to butt in where I wasn't invited."

"Smart boy. Now that you're here, you may as well have a look."

We walked over to the room at the other end of the basement and Quent closed the door and locked it behind us. Inside were a lot of conduit in the walls, reams of paper with numbers and equations, and an apparatus that looked like a cross between one of those fun-house mirrors and one of Quent's refracting machines from his office, with both hooked into a big computer against the wall. That strange glow came from a section of the mirror that collected the light from a projector into a strange pattern, like a fog that sits at the bottom of a valley. Being the type who can usually figure what something is by its design, I was surprised I had no idea what it was.

"Well?" he said. "What do you think?"

"What is it?" I said. A new thing to measure for contacts, maybe?"

"Not even close," he replied. "Something much more interesting than that, if I can work out the kinks." Then he got a faraway look in his eyes, and didn't say anything for awhile. I had gotten to know him well enough to not interrupt him when he got like that.

Presently he said, "Ray, what is the one thing us talking monkeys have been looking for since we climbed down out of the trees? The one thing most sought after by our species but never found?"

Now, normally I am not one to get into esoteric philosophy. Seems to me if the Great Inventor had meant for us to know the meaning of it all, It would have Its own page on Facebook where we could chat with It and get the answers we wanted. Since He didn't, I assumed such things were not our business. I said something about being clueless about anything that wasn't in a physic's book, but that I was interested in this odd machine.

Quentin sighed. "What is the one thing humans have not been able to do despite being able to build computers and spaceships and bathrooms? What is the one thing we can't even agree about going about trying to find?"

I guess I just looked stupid, because before I could come up with an answer he dove right in. "I'll tell you. After five million years, humans have learned to just about get by and figure out basic ways to stay alive, keep warm, come in out of the rain, and not kill each other over those things. Well, almost, anyway......but we can design a space shuttle but not really know what it is within us that allows us to do it. We can paint a Mona Lisa, but don't know why we choose this color or that. We make war, we make love, and we often find it hard to understand the difference between the two. In short, we don't know who or what we really are!"

"Oh, we've got the usual scientific explanations," he went on, "like it's all accidental chemical interactions that over time involved us setting up residence in a synapse somewhere between one neuron and another. Or, the religious ones that say we have a soul inside the body that nobody really agrees where it is, where it comes from, or where it goes to after we die. Or worst of all, that we are somehow a hotel for the devil where we have to pay the price for Adam's fondness for fruit. Sunday School Science, mystical opinion nobody knows about for sure, or great-grandchild to the amoeba. Right."

At that point I was too surprised to speak. Old Quent seemed to be the ultimate practical type, with no more use for an unprovable assumption than a chicken has for whether the egg came first or not. But he kept talking and got more worked up by the minute, going on about how we look in the mirror and have never had any idea what we were actually looking at. About the only thing I ever thought about when I looked in the mirror was how to un-invent the pimple. I thought at the time that the doc didn't have many people in his life he could go off like this with. Margo's interests never went past food, money, and the beauty salon, so I played along.

Quentin rolled on. "We ought to be ashamed of ourselves: we can map the atmospheric values on a planet a hundred light-years away but we don't know how consciousness hooks into the brain! Sure, thoughts are electrical impulses: that's how, but what about what? Looking in the brain for the self is like looking into a telescope to find God! I've had enough, Ray. For the last thirteen years I've been working on a machine that will answer these questions once and for all, by inventing a mirror that will reflect not just your face but your true and actual real nature and essence!"

About then, I was sure old Quent had been unzipped all this time and I hadn't noticed. Either that or he had found Margo's stash for her vodka and had been raiding it. I wasn't afraid or anything but I guess I kind of backed away a half-step, and he noticed it.

"I know what you're thinking. Old Quentin Blome is ready for some Thorazine. I don't expect you to take my word for it. 'Take my word for it' is what the pope and the professors demand. I intend to prove it, Ray. It wouldn't be good science for me to be the first subject, so I planned to use Margo all along. I've made all her glasses over the years, and made all the appropriate measurements for her particular set-up. I think I'm ready for a test run in a few weeks."

I said, "Hey doc, you don't have to prove anything to me. But what's the governing dynamic? What is it that makes it work, to do, what you say it will do?"

"Spoken like a true inventor! Ever try to look in a mirror with both eyes at once?"

I guess I wrinkled my forehead trying to visualize it.

"Don't blow a fuse, you can't. Our visual apparatus only allows us to triangulate, where both our eyes can only focus on a single object or view at a time. We can't look at two objects with each of our eyes simultaneously. The only way to look at both our eyes at once is to look at the bridge of the nose and see them peripherally. It is my opinion that if we could look into both our eyes directly, eye to eye in a mirror without having to triangulate or peripherate, we would finally see into ourselves and finally know the score about who and what we are!"

"But how do you get around the visual system limits?" I asked.

"By making some measurements first: interocular distance, height of eye level above the floor, focal length for your particular eyes, pupillary size ranges, depth of field, corneal curve, ocular muscle tension, pressure readings in the interior of the eyeball, etc. I load all those into the computer with a program I wrote, and based on the algorithms I've come up with, I grind a curve into a mirrored quartz surface that locks in your personal ocular system so that light traveling back to your eyes from the mirror is reflected directly back into its correlate in both of your pupils. I call it BORS, for Bilateral Optical Reflection Simultaneity. The ability to see inside yourself by looking into both your eyes in the same moment!"

Now, I knew a little about optics, and obviously old Quent knew what he was talking about when he talked about the eyes and how they worked. But the specific effect he claimed would occur even if he could lock in the BORS or whatever, was a bit much for me to swallow, and I said so.

He was silent for a long time. "I know what you mean, Ray. I don't know if this will work, but at least it's a new idea, and one that uses a system whose results can be easily replicated by others, instead of relying on belief, faith, or intuitive and esoteric analyses. Obviously human beings are some combination of physical and metaphysical: that much many poeple agree on. Maybe this is the way to getting it."

I said that that made sense to me. And by then his enthusiasm had gotten to me and I was hooked. My only fear was that he wouldn't let me in on it now that he'd talked with me about it. He must have read that in my eyes because he said I could hang around if I didn't bother him with too many idiot questions.

The next few weeks are a blur for me. All I can remember is that I spent every evening down in the workshop with Quentin, absorbing as much as I could while I held a piece of the machine in place while he secured it, or read to him from his notes, or just cleaned up after we were done for the night. As the day for the first trial came closer, the doc got more and more agitated. Even Margo let up a bit on her carping shrew thing then: she knew better than to pick at him when he was like that.

Finally the day came when it was ready.

The machine itself was in three pieces: one where the subject stood on a short platform that curved upwards behind them into a canopy-like overhang from which the headgear apparatus was suspended and into which the subject fit their eyes; the second, a curved mirror ground into a piece of quartz mounted on a movable adjustable upright to allow for differing heights of eye level that was connected to the platform on an adjustable track set about 3 meters away; and third, a computer-linked control panel that governed a laser light source above the headgear, and from which the doc could make micro-adjustments in the mirror's angulation.

All in all it was fairly crude, but all Quentin wanted to do with this prototype was to illustrate the basic SBOR principle in real time and see what happened. If it worked, he would of course license out manufacture of a more sophisticated unit.

After dinner that night, Quentin went down to make some last minute adjustments and then worked to convince Margo to come down to the man-cave and have a look at what he had been working on, which was no small task. She didn't like going down into a smelly low-ceiling dank place where spider webs could tangle up in her 'do. After assuring her all she had to do was step up on the platform, put her eyes in the headgear, and look into the mirror when it illuminated, she reluctantly agreed, all the while treating us to her usual tirade about all the sacrifices she had made for him over the years.

"Now what did you say this horrid thing is supposed to do?" she snipped. "Quentin, you know my heart can't take....."

"Nonsense. You're fine. The doctor gave you a clean bill of health just last month."

"What does he know? Anyway, it's dusty down here. I think I feel my allergy coming on, and when that happens you know my migraines start .... ."

"Don't worry, don't worry .... all you have to do is stand there, and when the light comes on, look at the mirror and tell me what you see," Quentin replied, holding his exasperation to a minimum.

"How much did all of this cost? Quentin Blome, if you've been spending our money without telling me where .... ."

"Margo, please....the sooner we do this the sooner you can go back upstairs and get back to your complete DVD set of *Lost*, OK?"

"Oh, all right. But be quick about it. Can you believe that Nikki and Paulo .... ."

"OK Margo, here we go," Quentin said from behind the control panel. "Three, two, one, now!" The strange light glowed in the mirror, and Margo looked directly into it.

She looked, went still, then tore off the headgear and ran screaming from the room.

She was out on the front lawn running toward the street by the time Quent and I caught up to her, and at that, we had to tackle her from going any further. She was hollering incoherently, and nothing we said got through to her. After a few minutes of unsuccessful attempts to calm her down, the doc figured it was best to get her to the ER. I agreed, as Quentin looked pretty grim himself. And the doctor hadn't given him a clean slate.

They sedated her at the hospital, which at least stopped her shrieking. But the silence that followed was even worse. She got that glossy-eyed stare so common in catatonia, like she was looking at something no one else could see, or would want to. They kept her for about two weeks, but there was no change, and the doc had a hell of a time trying to explain what happened without giving away the secret of the BORS unit. They couldn't find anything wrong physically with Margo, so Quent and I knew the effect of the unit was not something that harmed the body. But obviously and clearly it affected the mind.

After a few days they sent her to a facility better suited to treat what they wound up calling a nonspecific hysterical conversion reaction. As far as I know, she is still there.

Quentin didn't say a word for days, after which he went on a vodka binge of his own that lasted the better part of three weeks. I took an unofficial semester break from school, both to keep the house in a semblance of order and make sure the doc was kept an eye on, in between the son coming home to take care of the things I couldn't.

After almost a month, Quent climbed out of his black hole and rejoined the living. Then came a day or two of tears before he finally started to talk. "Ray, " he said, "I don't know what happened down there to poor Margo, but it's my fault. I never should have tried it on her. The only way to make up for it is to try it myself and figure out what happened. That way maybe I can help the doctors help her."

That was what I was afraid he was going to say, and I tried to protest, saying what good could he do her if the same thing happened to him?

But he wouldn't have any of it. "I've got to know what she saw. Maybe if I see it, I can help her come back."

There was just no arguing with him. He had sobered up enough to want to do it right then and there, so we went down to the unit, and made all the adjustments for his own optical setup to make the thing work for him. He had me work the control panel, and to this day I don't know why I helped him, other than I was in a follow-orders mode trying to help him, and of course the whole experience had kicked me in the gut too.

As he stepped onto the platform, I tried to talk him out of it one last time. But he just turned and looked me with his eyes blazing with fear, pain, and resolute determination. He didn't say a word. I started the countdown.

When the moment of truth came, Quentin looked at the strange light in the mirror, and said nothing. From where I was standing, I could see him turn his head quizzically one way, then the next. I don't know how long he stood there, but I remember thinking he shouldn't do it much longer for fear the light could damage his retinas. Finally after what seemed like an eternity, he removed the apparatus, and stepped off the platform.

I realized then I had been holding my breath. "Doc, Quentin, are you okay?"

He was staring out at nothing the same way Margo had, and I had to ask him twice to get him pulled out of it. "Huh? Oh .... hello, Ray. Yes, yes, I'm fine. Never better." He was wearing a strange half-smile that didn't give away any information at all.

I was going crazy, of course. "So what did you see? What was it that happened to Margo? Why didn't it do it to you? Are you sure you're okay?"

"Oh," he said nonchalantly. "It's not important. Nothing here is of any importance now. Here, help me bust this thing up." Unable to get anything more out of him, I followed orders again, and we took apart in a few hours what had taken him thirteen years to build.

When it was done, he burned all his notes in the fireplace and made me promise never to tell anyone about what happened. Then he walked up the stairs, out the door, and to my knowledge has never been heard from since. Their son wound up setting Margo up in a longer-term facility, and I hear she's getting better, but has no memory of what happened in that basement. The police actually tried to get more out of me after the doc disappeared, but I played dumb convincingly enough. The BORS unit was completely dismantled so there wasn't anything to connect what happened to it.

Me, I switched majors after that, started a minor in computer programming, and now am in the last year at the State School of Optometry, busily learning everything I can about interocular distance, focal lengths, pupillary size ranges, depth of field readings, corneal curve, ocular muscle tension, and pressure readings of the eyeball. Whatever happened in that basement was worth pursuing, and even though I had years ahead of me trying to duplicate the doc's computer program algorithms, I remember a bit of what I learned helping him set it up, and am determined to find out what it is that he saw that made him walk away from his life and had whacked out Margo so badly.

I know he made me promise not to tell anyone, but with him gone, I had to tell someone now that I am trying to duplicate what he did.

If I succeed, I'll let you know.

See? I said that you wouldn't believe me.

Mandy

Never, ever am I ever going to get fooled again, Mandy said to herself, as she blew her nose loudly. What could I have been I thinking, letting Cal know so soon into things how much I always wanted him? Aaaarggghh .... why doesn't life have an erase and re-record button? Here I am seventeen and still acting like a clueless thirteen year old!

She laid back on her bed, hoping her mother wouldn't hear her crying and make a fuss about it .... she thought, whenever she finds me upset, she has to get all the 411 and then it's like I always have to take care of her so she feels better about me being upset. In that way it's like I'm the mother and like she's the daughter. It was a little better with Dad, but it was like he would just always shake his head and say all, 'Hey, I tried to tell you about guys, but you wouldn't listen.' Then he'd go back to doing his goddamn crosswords.

Mandy remembered when she was around twelve, when all the love and attention she got from Dad all her life suddenly stopped. She had always been Daddy's little princess, always up on his lap and cuddling, always holding hands when they did things. His big love and attention was something she somehow knew inside her made her mom upset. Maybe in some ways Dad did it to piss her mother off, who knows? It was like they all never seemed to agree about anything ever: it was like their life together was like a memory that faded away a long time ago.

But then with no word or warning at all, it was like I was beast or something, and Dad didn't want anything to do with me. I couldn't understand why he didn't love me the way he did before. The only thing he said was something like 'you're getting too big for all that.' Maybe it was because my breasts developed early, she thought, the envy of her girlfriends and the object of boy's attention because she was also so slim at the same time. But when her father had said she was getting too big for love, it made her resent her own body like there was something wrong with her. Her breasts made her feel ugly then, and she used to try to push them down at night to make them smaller so her Dad would want her on his lap again.

But then other times she would catch him looking at her really intense-like, and she knew he was looking at her 'that way.' But as soon as he saw that she saw, he turned away right then, pretending like it never happened. This both confused her and pleased her, but she could never figure out why it did both, why it gave her tingles in one way and made her feel ashamed too.

She remembered when she was fourteen and made out with a guy for the first time, Boyd from down the block: OMFG what a loser he turned out to be, but I was like all crazy in love with him at the time: kissing him was like the best thing ever. She remembered she was shocked when she felt him get all hard in his pants, but that made her feel like he loved me What a crock of shit! she said to herself, bringing on more fresh tears .... I used to think if a guy got hard and all when he made out with me, that meant he loved me! What a loser I am! All they want is to get off! How could I be so stupid? All they want is to grope and get what they want.

She turned over, wanting to masturbate to make herself feel better, but even that seemed like too much effort. Maybe I should call Carolyn, she thought .... no, she had always wanted Cal too: no help there. I fell in love with Cal when I was fifteen, like most of my friends. But unlike them, I never hit on him, just hoping he would see me and want me on his own.

Then, finally, after going with so many of my friends he asked me out. It felt so good to have his attention on me, and at first he didn't go for what he could get like the other guys. It was so slammin' to feel like he seemed to actually want to know what was important to me. That's why I wound up telling him how much I always loved and wanted him. That's when he made the moves, and 'cause it felt so good to finally be with him, I did what I did. I'd never gone to all those rainbow parties to hook up with guys like Carolyn, but I did the half-nasty with him, the first time with a guy. It was so exciting and I felt so good and close afterward, and he seemed so happy.

But then Monday, when he came over after school, I spilled all over him how much I had always wanted to be his girl and loved him from a distance. Then, the next day it was like, nobody's home and I felt beast again just like I did with my father, all dirty and confused and wishing I could take back all of it.

What is it with guys? First dad makes like he loves me forever and then all of a sudden it's my bad for wanting it to be the same as always. Then guys make it seem like they want you, but then it's always a game to get you to want them so they can get off. Then if you give away that you want or feel something more, it's like you don't exist.

She sat up in her bed abruptly.

Wait a minute, she thought: two can play at this. I've got a bitchin' body and my face isn't bad, a little like LiLo's. I'm so tired of being the nice girl too scared to hook up. I've got the goods, why not use them? Then I would be in control instead of the guy. Why not? They do shit to us, why can't we do the same? Isn't that being a good feminist, taking power for myself as a woman and not letting guys run me? Not being a victim and taking my own right to be strong? If they don't care about me, why should I care about them?

I'll use what I've got to get what I want. I'll cupcake Cal but play cool and drive him crazy until he drools for me, and even then I'll keep him on the hook until I am good and ready to let him have me. He knows it was good what we did last week. I can get him again easy if I want, if I play right. Or maybe I'll forget Cal for ignoring me and go for Chaz, who's even hotter than Cal. Too bad he's with that bitch Joanna. But I'm way hotter than her anyway, and smarter too.

For the first time in her life Mandy felt strong instead of confused. She smiled to herself and felt like a whole new world was beginning to open up to her.

Maybe it wouldn't be so bad to finally be the one with the power. Yeah!

Paul

When Paul had found out his guru had had sex with his 15 year-old daughter, one part of him felt inflated, that an enlightened master had chosen his own daughter for such a powerful transmission of shakti. But after a day or two, a darker aspect of himself had arose, enraged at the vision of the actual act, which kept coming up over and over. Like a good seeker and as he had been trained to do for so long, he had let both reactions arise without a secondary attachment or repulsion to either, watching them, giving them both room, and expecting them to dissipate.

Paul had always had doubts about his guru over the years, and a reluctant but persistent resistance to many aspects of the teaching and the overall ethos of the ashram. He was told these doubts were his ego holding on, their presence proof that the teaching was going in so far that it was creating deep resistance, and as such, said good things about him.

His wife Teresa could not give up her doubts, though, and she left him and the sangha after their daughter was born, telling him one day he would wake up and see what kind of game was being played on him in the name of enlightenment. He had replied that it was she who resisted waking up, and that he would not leave when he had finally met a truly enlightened teacher and had a chance to make the Great Leap inward, then outward, and finally not-ward.

But now his doubts started to renew themselves powerfully.

Had Teresa been right all along?

After a time, no matter how much he tried to give it meditative room to ventilate, the darker rageful part would not yield to the impermanency of ever-ephemeral arising illusion of the self. It planted itself squarely in his third chakral chi and would not move, growing in energy and emotion over the past week. He wondered if the persistency of the responses meant he had some hidden father-daughter lust thing going on that brought jealousy and drove his resentment.

His guru had said countless times that the enlightened teacher or teaching is never wrong, that it was always the student that was wrong, so it made sense to look for the shadow within him.

In that way, Paul had always been taught that when there was attachment to an emotive reaction of that magnitude that would not let go through witnessing, meditation, and time, it meant that part of the illusory self was strongly holding out to be real. In such a case, the guru taught that for a time it was best to talk to that aspect until it felt assuaged and comforted, and then it would eventually let go into the Sunyata that every thing and not-thing is.

Paul had once asked him if such a technique was a kind of a manipulation, lulling the attached part into a warm recognition only to later pull the reality of its existence out from under it. The guru had laughed, saying that was just the therapist in him talking and that it was the opposite, that that part of the ego was trying to manipulate him into feeling sorry for it so it could stay believing it was real, when in the end both he and it were all illusions anyway.

When Paul asked how an illusion could have the power to manipulate him, the guru just laughed even more. He went on to say that seekers in the west were always inappropriately wanting to do psychotherapy in sangha, and Paul had been instructed to spend extra time in meditation in order to let that piece of the ego go.

But this ever-deepening rage would not respond to his attempts at meditative amelioration, would not speak to him, and only had one dominant emotive gestalt: to kill. When he shared it with Bishe, Paul's closest friend in the zendo, Bishe commented that this part of his ego was really angry at the guru for trying to help Paul be rid of ego for the last twenty-two years, and that now it had an outlet for that resentment, it wanted to do to the guru what the guru had been trying to do to it for all those years.

For this reason, Bishe, the heir apparent to the guru who was closer to enlightenment than all the others, had said to just continue to sit with that and that it would dissipate over time. Paul could feel what his ego wanted to say in response to that, but did not share it.

What Paul didn't know was that Bishe had gone straight to the guru with what he had been told. As expected, the guru gave it only a cursory dismissive response.

In addition to the rage, Paul was also racked with personal guilt, but couldn't tell if that was his chi speaking or he. He tried to let the guilt arise and ventilate, but the more he focused on it the more its voice tortured him. It said, 'You brought her here after the divorce when Teresa didn't want to stay. You handed her to him. You gave up your father role and transferred it to him. You have a dark sexual secret of your own about your daughter that makes you jealous. You abnegated your responsibility as a parent and look what happened. Teresa was right: You are the one who has been asleep.'

He wanted to talk to his daughter about it all but didn't have a chance, what with the women and the men in different parts of the ashram, and also because she was put in isolation after the blessed event to be able to digest and let the experience move through her and give it a chance to open her up to new vistas of consciousness. All the women who had been given the honor of receiving the master that way underwent the same kind of process.

In the midst of this personal torture had then come the incomprehensible news. They had just discovered that his daughter had hanged herself in her room. His precious daughter was dead by her own hand. Horror piled on torture .... this was too much, he thought, too much .... could this really be happening? It was more like soap-opera drama than real life.

By the time he got to her room she had been taken down and placed in her bed. The room was full of people in quiet but intense communion, and as they parted to let him through to her, many murmured to him that she must have been so enraptured by the experience with the teacher that in an ecstatic state she may have wanted to be rid of the shackles of the bodymind and so decided to break the bondage and be free forever.

At first, Paul was numb from the overwhelm, struggling to make it all real. He had heard all the commiseration, but when he got back to his own room after okaying arrangements for cremation, the numbness wore off, and something moved inside, like a tumbler clicking into place that began unlocking something ancient and foreboding, both alien and familiar. Then the dark aspect in his chi finally exploded and engulfed him. All the years of repressed doubt detonated from the spark of his daughter's death.

In one gestalt, each and every experience in the zendo shifted in his mind from one orientation to another. Where before there was a smiling guru extolling how all their personal reactivities were the product of an ego holding on for dear life, there was now only a sneering despot making sure all resistance was either shamed or blamed as a pathology of consciousness, with no room for any real discourse or open-ended outcome to that discourse from anyone, using a two-and-half millennium-old point-of-view to weld the system shut.

There was enough awareness in him to imagine that this picture was what Teresa saw all along and he didn't, and that thought made him feel truly suicidal. Even so, he was also marginally enough aware that this picture still could be his ego inventing a scenario so as to not submit to the Truth. But nothing could stop the roaring freight train of his rage. It was like someone else had taken over his body and he could do nothing to stop it.

As in a dream, later that evening he was barely able to watch himself sneak into the armory in the second sublevel of the zendo that only he and a few other trusted seekers knew about, pick up a handgun in the storeroom stocked for the end times, stow it in his robes, and walk resolutely to the guru's personal quarters.

He gave a pretext to the guru's circle of handlers, and because Paul was a long time resident and had been given private audience without notice before, the handlers checked with the teacher, assuming he needed some guidance about his daughter's recent liberation. The teacher agreed and they let him pass.

He found his teacher lounging in his gold pajamas on his spotless white divan. Behind him Paul locked the door so quietly it went unnoticed. The guru looked up and smiled.

"Hello, Paul. I hear it is hard for you right now."

Again, as in a dream because Paul had never spoken to his teacher like this before, he said, "Yes, but it will get even harder for one of us." With that, he pulled out the gun, and let his arm hold it at his side. The guru eyed the ordinance with a special attentiveness, but remained outwardly calm.

Patting the divan, he said, "Come, sit with me and we'll talk."

Paul shook his head, and the dark energy in his chi began to emerge. With an evenness exactly in measure to the volcano simmering within and so expressing and not repressing its power, he said, "There's nothing to talk about. There is only what is."

The guru narrowed his eyes. "And what is it that is?"

"That someone will die because of what you have done."

"What 'I' have done? What 'I' is that?"

"You know exactly what I mean."

"I know exactly what you think your 'I' means, but I have no idea what your 'I' thinks my 'I' did."

"Enough enlightenment talk. It's time for liberation," and he pointed the gun at him.

The teacher laughed, but not completely in energetic control. "I am already liberated. What are you talking about?"

"So you have no interest in either living or dying?"

"I only have interest in the *question* of living and dying, and not the answer."

"So it doesn't matter to you whether I choose to shoot you?"

"No one chooses anything, everything just happens. What you call me and what you call you are just arbitrary contrivances of arising passingness."

Paul replied, "So the trigger pulls itself?"

"The trigger is pulled by that which does not choose, but acts."

"How does something act without someone choosing to activate the act?"

"Only someone who believed in and was enslaved by ego would ask this question."

Paul grunted in loud frustration, cocked the trigger on the gun, and touched the barrel of the gun to the guru's nose. "So there isn't someone in there who cares if you live or die?"

"I live and die every arising moment in concert with the objects of my awareness. What is the difference if the bullet decides to make that living and dying occur in another way?"

"She was my daughter, you son-of-a-bitch! You used her for your own gratification and left her no room to do anything but kill herself because there was no other way for her to deal with you using your power with her to get what you wanted!"

"She was not 'your' daughter. She was not a victim to my power. She chose ..... ."

"Oh, so now there's such a thing as choice, when it's convenient for you to need it?"

"This was always your problem, interrupting the teacher .... ."

"Don't sidestep the issue! You said 'she chose.' I'm warning you, answer the question!"

"The dove does not inspire, nor the vulture offend."

Paul pulled the gun away from the guru's face and went nose-to-nose with him. "That's what you always do! Use a koan when someone traps you in the content of your own contradictive bullshit!" He then head-butted him hard, leaving the teacher's nose bloody.

Dabbing at his bleeding nose, the teacher remained calm. "This is the ego talking. The ego does not like it when it is confronted. Your violence against the one who is trying to help you get beyond it, proves what I am trying to tell you is true."

Paul ran his hand frustratedly through his hair and paced in a slow circle around the lushly appointed room.

"So since there is no self, there is no such thing as what we call self-responsibility?"

"There is only that which arises, and That Which allows that which arises, to arise."

"So you have no regret about what you did with her because without a self, there is no self-responsibility, and you raping her was just what was arising?"

"She was not raped, but what you say is essentially correct."

"So there is no you, but actions arise. Those actions just act and seek whatever object they seek, without you. When they find the object they seek, that object does not choose to respond, it just has its own reactive arising to the first arising that activated it. Then each co-arising allows itself to be taken to an outcome decided not by any chooser but by That Which allows them to arise in the first place."

The guru clapped his hands once. "Yes!"

"And so there is no room for emotion, for caring, for connecting with others, or for feeling how others feel about how we treat them?"

"All such emotion is just the self justifying its attractions and repulsions to itself, the snake always trying to swallow its own tail to define itself so it can go on living. Emotions are simply a subset of mind: when the mind releases, so do emotions."

"What about other lineages of Buddhism that retain personally embodied emotive forms of love and connection with people after enlightenment?"

"Buddha taught us that it is not that the self needs to be extinguished, but that the self was actually never born in the first place. Other lineages that promote a self's devotional or connected relatedness with Others or gods of some kind, simply do not abide with the true teaching in its purest essence and expression. Expressing the truest love for someone is shown by not supporting their ego and its attachments to illusion."

"But didn't Siddhartha talk about the Great Compassion, not just in context of not supporting ego, but in the content of everyday life? Where is the post-enlightenment compassion in your world?"

"The Great Compassion arises when there is no self in the way to limit its expression."

"Where was the Great Compassion arising when you were not feeling how being raped felt to my daughter?"

"Nothing can ever be known, only experienced. The body wanted what the body wanted."

"So you didn't experience any felt emotion about how what you did felt to her?"

"I do not have experience. Experience has me. She did not have experience, experience had her, whether she was conscious of this truth or not."

"What if her body didn't want it, but she was too afraid to make you stop because you have had such power over her since she was an infant, she couldn't resist, which was my fault because I brought her here in the first place?"

"You holding onto believing anything, or thinking you know the experience of anyone else, or that anything is your fault, is only your ego insisting to exist."

"I've heard that all before. Answer the question."

"Her world was her world. But my world is not my world. When the world of one who isn't touches the world of one who insists on being, life arises with new challenges that can be danced to or not. I cannot speak to what her body wanted. That is neither a world of mine nor a world of yours."

"So you do have a world that is yours?"

"The only world that is mine is the one that can never be mine."

"So the only thing in 'your' world was what your body wanted, with no concern for what she wanted?"

"The only thing was what this body wanted, not my body. Her body had its own language and interpretations of experience, one way or another. It wanted what it wanted or didn't want, and in the end, it wanted to end itself, and so it did."

Paul stopped abruptly and stared at his teacher. He realized in that moment that neither the sexual act nor her death registered in any significant way in his consciousness. Nothing did. For him life was a continuously flowing river with no beginning and no end, and he only noticed the part that got his feet wet, and then only for a moment before it was gone. He wavered within for a moment, getting his first real taste of what enlightenment entailed.

But just as quickly the face of his dead daughter returned to him. His forehead tightened, and then his face cleared slowly but markedly, and something energetic substantively released from him and his whole body changed its energy. The guru, tracking the subtle musculature in his face, noticed this and relaxed somewhat.

With a newly attained calm, Paul said, "So the body that is not yours, wanted the body that was not hers, with no mind in the arising of whether or not the body that was not hers wanted to receive the body that was not yours?"

"That is correct."

Paul smiled, but not a happy smile. "I think I am finally starting to get it. I think I am finally onto your whole enlightened perspective. So that is the way it is, after enlightenment?

"Yes, yes, yes!"

"And that is the great freedom accorded by leaving the ego's story of itself?"

"Yes!"

"To know that all consciousness is a function of a Buddhanature where one can't experience the experiencer of experience, only experience what the experiencer experiences?"

"Yes!" said the guru. I can't believe it, he thought to himself. Could this ego actually be breaking through?

"And so because there is no self, there is never any self-responsibility, no one home inside who ever has to feel that anything is their fault, able to allow all actions to arise without personal authorship, with no ethical destination except the trust that That Which Is knows best where It wants to go?"

"Always and ever!"

"That no one else's reality matters to you because there is no real 'them' having a reality and no you that has to care about their no-reality, making all connection with other people a dance of illusion by illusional selves?"

"As I have said, so many times."

"So there can never really be any real love between people because there are no such things as selves that would feel the love they have for one another was real?"

"Only when we see through to all the personal attachments to personal love we grip to so tightly does the Great Freedom find us and replace the need for the craving of love."

Paul stared at his teacher wide-eyed and said, "That is what I have given my whole life over to? To a place where love is just an illusory grab of one illusory self for another illusory self? Where relational space with others is moot? To a state where an empty source comes from nowhere, is nowhere, ends up nowhere? Where there is no cause and no effect to human life? That is the meaning of Buddhism and the true enlightened life?"

The guru smiled self-satisfyingly. "What we call Love is never personal, only universal. Real connection is never personal, only universal. So in the purest way of speaking, everything you are saying is in accordance with the teaching."

Paul shook his head. "Even if what you say is true on one level, it isn't on all levels. To teach this kind of anti-personal crap as the total answer to everything in all domains turns people into robots programmed by what they think and taught as absolute truth, making them float up and off their own humanity, all the while bleating like baby sheep to get the attention and approval of the parent wolf."

The teacher sighed: again comes the wall to the Truth. "That's just the ego talking again, justifying his refusal to submit."

"Maybe. Or maybe you are talking from the ego of one claiming to have no ego, justifying its own fears of really inhabiting its own emotive-based humanity, unenlightened warts and all."

Paul sighed deeply, looking at the gun. "This all has to end .... now is as good a time as any, yes?" He looked up and stared at the guru with neither kindness nor malevolence, then looked at the gun.

"One bullet, with no cause, but certainly with some effect." He paused and sighed again. "I guess a bullet is not enlightened."

The he put the gun on his temple, then pointed it at the teacher, then back to his temple, back to the teacher, back to his temple, back to the teacher again.

When the handlers heard the single shot they raced to the door, found it locked, and began to pound on it, yelling.

Madigan's

Aldo Vallone walked into Madigan's bar in Boston's Southie area after finishing his shift at the construction site, and saw his friend and co-worker Tom McGowan sitting at the bar. Pointing to Tom, he called out to the bartender, "Heya Colin, when did you staht serving Irish trash like that in here?"

"This here's a Mick bar, ya dumb Dago," replied the bartender. "And greaseball Italians always gotta pay extra."

"Oh, yeah I forgot .... ," he replied as he sat down smiling next to Tom. "So where were ya today, Tomba? The foreman weren't too happy about you being gahne. Had to get someone else quick at time-and-a half."

"Whaddaya have, wop?" Colin asked as he sidled up to them.

"Same as always, ya Mick bastard: a dahk beer."

"Whut, no pansy-ass chardonnay today for yuz?"

"Hey, ya balmy bog-trotter, just cuz you got no class don't mean the rest of us don't."

"Class, he sez," Colin replied, "as he wahlks in here with a black leather jacket and a pinkie ring."

"Hey, I like this ring," Aldo replied. "My uncle Louie gave it to me before he died."

".... of terminal Wop-itis, for sure," said Colin as he moved to get him his beer.

"So?" said Aldo, as he turned back to Tom.

"Ah hell, Aldo .... me and Dottie had a big blowup last night and I just couldn't get the juice to work today."

"Same ol'-same ol'?"

"Nah, something different this time. She says her fahciitator be sayin' that ahr codependence is gettin' worse 'cause I don't open up enough to how she's feelin,' at the same time I expect her to open up to what I'm feelin,' callin' me a macho asshole cuz of it."

"Jeez, Tommer .... I thought yuz two had that figured awhile back.

You know as the meat-hangers we guys gotta go the extra mile in that openin' up depahtment."

"Aye .... but ahm havin' trouble trackin' my defense's cahmpensations, especially when ahm too fah into mine own closed-off picturah of reahlity."

"Is yer fourth chakra opened up enough when yuz two make love?"

"Hell no, not yet .... my fahcilitator tells me that ain't gonna happen til I get me ma outta my life once and for ahl."

"Well yuz can take that to the bank, Tommy-boy. She's poison for ya. She still thinks yer nine years old, the way she talks to ya. And they way she hates a great girl like Dottie like she wuz trash, that just ain't right by any stretch."

"Give it a name .... but now that my da's in the ground, it's hahd to say no, ya know? She's been drinkin' hahd since the funeral, and with me bein' the only kid around any more, all the shite falls to me."

"Has your fahcilitator talked to you about caretakin'? Shit, mine's got a litany goin' about that for me. Got me to see that if I don't pre-construct a safe space for love, ahm afraid Bella won't love me back, and that's a defended way to not feel vulnerable."

"Vulnerable .... ?" said Colin as he brought up Aldo's beer. "Whaddaya ya guys talkin' about? Are yuz two so pussy-whipped by yuz wimmen they got yuz goin' soft now?"

Aldo looked forlornly at him. "Colin, you know .... some day, some life yer gonna have to git with the program and staht lookin' at how yer whole thing with broads is just a cover for not facin' into how you're really a cake-boy deep down, capishe?"

Colin laughed. "That comin' from a guy who still goes to confession with guys who wear dresses. And I stahted workin' last month with someone, that's how much yuz know, dago-boy. "

"Hey, that's great Colin! It's about time yuz did something about yer life. But it's called reconciliation now, not confession, ya dumb Mick. And no, I don't go no more to church. I found out in facilitation that was only a way to keep mah low self-worth fed full with fuck-me food from the pope."

"Christ, Aldo .... it took ya this long to figure that out, did it? Goddam friggin' can't ever trust those pansies with ahr kids when they sell out their balls for Jesus, and when all they's care about is lookin' like they're right and good, and not 'bout whut really be true fer true."

"Fuhgeddaboutit," said Aldo. "Burn it all down and let all the gypsies kicked outta France move to the Vatican, I says. Now that'd be some fun beautiful thang."

"Are you sayin' yuz stopped bein' such a stingy Mick and finally be payin' for some help for yuz heart-space, Colin?" said Tom.

"Sure, sure .... this way now I can be a real help to all yuz boozers who come in here cryin' like bonnie lasses about yuz poor pathetic lives, right?"

"Fokkin'-ay Colin .... ' Aldo replied. "Ya think now yuz gonna hold up your dyahdic half-pahrt of relation space with ahl of us here in the joint?"

"Ah'll sure be holdin' up my end with yuz all. Yuz just be makin' sure yer own noodles is cooked before you go and sayin' mine b'ain't," Colin said with a smile.

"Aye," said Tom. "Only be careful with Aldo here callin' his pasta the likes of noodles. He be goin' all Corleone on yer arse fer that."

"Ah, yuz got me all shakin' in me wee boots."

"Hey Colin, turn up the boob box a bit, will ya?" Aldo said as he heard something on the TV over the bar.

The bartender obliged, as the announcer was saying, ".....as far as we can tell, Sharon, the audio checks out authentic. It's Bin Laden for sure. It looks he's just sent a message to the White House saying he's realized all of his rage against America was just a projection of his unhealed authority issues, and that 9/11 was only his way to express his rage against a father who never noticed him. Sources tell us that the Taliban will now begin withdrawing from most of the tribal areas they now hold and start to .... ."

"Well ah'll be a goddamned kangaroo in heat," said Aldo. "That fokkin' camel-jockey finally got it, huh? Wot's gonna happen now, ya think? Maybe now the shite be slowin' down in the sandbox, huh?"

"And maybe ahr lads can finally get outta Afgoonistan and come home," said Tom.

"Ah'll drink to that," Colin said. He raised his voice to everyone in the lounge. "Hey ya bloody boozehounds, Bin Laden's hangin' up his hard-on with the U.S. of A.! Says his da is the reason he's been such a shite-head all along. Suds is on the house for the next ten minutes!"

A raucous "About fokkin' time!" went up in the bar, with the line forming fast at the tap.

"Hey, yuz think Osama-Bama'll finally come outta the raghead closet now?" said Tom.

"Ah, ya still holdin' onta that one, Tom?" Colin said. "Everyone knows he be a Scientologer all along, and his parents be space aliens."

"Well, with Michelle holdin' the stones in that relationship, it don't really matter, now does it?" replied Aldo. "The boss is the one who lets the other one be boss. One day she be learnin' to put away the dick, and he be wakin' up to his pussy-boy playin.'"

"And spreadin' his legs wide for them Wall street wankers, letting 'em go on the dole on our dime without cleanin' up their own houses first and dumpin' the do-ers," added Colin.

"Amen to both of yuz," said Tom. "We's may be well had Hilary-dilary in there all along."

"Aye," said Colin. "With Billy-boy packin' his pants as he be, she be always carryin' stones of her own to even it up, by God. She shoulda been the one in there runnin' things all along, I says. I'da voted fer her twice if I coulda, just like in the old days."

Tom, raised his glass and said, "To lads who be packin' and lasses who be rackin'!"

"Hey now," replied Aldo. "Careful 'bout shovelin' that shit-on-a-stick, Tommy-boy. Now ya gotta tell Dottie ya laid out that low consciousness dick-boy diddle in front of ahl of us, so's nothin's hid, right? She's gotta know, ya know."

"Ah shite, yuz right, Aldo. Ah be shamin' on that one, fer sure," said Tom, shaking his head. "And on the couch fer a week, prob'ly. I gotta git that macho prick Sentinel outta me once and fer ahl."

Aldo continued, "That's right, Tomala: he's just the compensation in ya for how yer ma kept ya down and beholdin' to her all yer life, so's now that part de-humanizes women all sexual-like to get some power fer hisself. You gotta get more muscles than him fer sure or Dottie's gonna be through with ya some day, and that'd be nuttin' but nuttin' but right then. The time's now for men and women to get how each got their own place strong and heartful all equal-like."

Aldo paused, raised his own glass and said, "To a world where men and women and micks and wops and ragheads and spades and honkies and chinks and nips and bohunks and beaners and huns and yids and people and animals all get along on this little blue planet! In the end, each other's all we got .... !"

But before they could complete the toast, Colin raised his glass, and spoke loudly to the entire bar now listening, "May your neighbors respect ye .... trouble neglect ye .... the angels protect ye .... and heaven accept ye!"

"Hoo-yah!"

Larry

My God, Larry thought as he sat alone on the living room sofa in one of his usual silent musings. I can't believe how quick time is passing these days. Mandy is growing up so fast, and turning out to be so beautiful. It's been almost eight months since I had to change things between us, and now it's like I'm more alone than ever.

God, if she only knew that Lisa and I only got married because Lisa was pregnant with her, she would be heartbroken. We never told her, and made her think her birthday happened a year later. Lisa and I have had to work hard to make her think we still love each other so she never suspects the truth about how things really are. Time enough for that when she is older.

I convinced myself that it was the right thing to do at the time, of course: my father beat into us kids that a man never runs away from his responsibilities to women and children. But we had only known each other about four months, and we were just kids ourselves, for God's sake. But what else was there to do? Lisa refused to even consider getting an abortion because her Catholic parents would have disowned her.

God forbid she'd lose her idiot mommy and daddy! What a couple of dunskies .... what sane person could go along with what one had to believe in order to be a Catholic? How could you have an IQ more than 70 and believe that the bread on the altar actually, and not symbolically, turned into Jesus's flesh after the eunuch in robes up there did his abba-dabba-do thing, and the wine actually, and not symbolically, turned into Jesus's blood too? What do they call it .... ? Transub-something, that the flesh and blood thing is real, not symbolic, and that if you don't believe it you can't be a good Catholic. And if you don't believe it as a Catholic, it's a sin. Probably a mortal one, in their thing.

This is the twenty-first century, for God's sake. And if the boys in the red dresses and the guy in the tall white hat in Rome teach this kind of magic crap, how could anyone possibly take seriously anything else they stood for? Especially with what they did to Galileo and Da Vinci, the Inquisisiton, all the child abuse they consciously covered up over all the years, and how Vatican City is the only country in the modern world where, by law, the age of sexual consent is twelve.

How can no one connect the dots on that one?

Unbelievable.

Thank God my parents were Lutheran. I loved being Lutheran: a laid-back religion for people who don't want to work up too much sweat about God. Everything is clean and polite and harmless. But Martin Luther, what a guy! The man was a lion .... I don't think he ever imagined he'd wind up starting up such a vanilla white toast religion like Lutheranism when he had the kind of stones to post those points on that cathedral door.

But I'm sure glad he did. Those bastards in Rome deserved it then just like they deserve the shit-storm happening now in all the news about their conscious centuries-old program of cover-ups for the pedophilia, a practice that was acceptable enough in their corporate culture to simply play a shell game with the abusers, rather than to take eradicative steps centuries before they were forced to by modern communication and discourse.

The best part of that 2012 disaster movie with another version of John Cusack's Everyman was seeing St. Peter's basilica collapse on all the cardinals and roll over and crush all the idiot papists in the square!

It really would be a better world if they were gone. Sell all the jewels, paintings and real estate, give all the money away to the poor they say they want to help but save some back for forced penilectomies for all the molesters, and then make all the priests, bishops, nuns, and cardinals get real jobs, I say. Make the pope have to work at a 7-11 in inner city Detroit and share two nightshifts a week with Achmed, and then see how much love and compassion for mankind he has left.

But British Petroleum would probably headhunt him for their Department of Incompetence, Posturing, and Lies first. Or better yet, the Republicans would want him to run for president, with Palin as his perfect VP. That way when she got tired of being vice-president and quit like she likes to do when she gets in one of her trailer park snits, the pope could name Dr. Laura to replace her.

Now that's what I'd call an apocalypse .... beam me up, Scotty!

But when Mandy came along, I was completely surprised by how I reacted to her. Never before had I ever felt loved like she loved me. I had thought my life was over, doomed to be a slave to some drooling child and idiot wife that would rob me of all my dreams. But she was so alive and precocious right from the start, so unlike Lisa in all her sullen moodiness. Everything was an adventure for Mandy, and it reminded me of how my own life used to be so full of shiny promise. I loved her like I loved no other person in my whole life, and I felt loved by her like no other person had ever loved me, even if she was a child.

We became fast friends, Mandy and I, and it felt so good to be part of something that seemed to be such a gift for both of us. Too bad if Lisa felt left out: she chose to be out of it herself, preferring to complain all the time about getting fat while she drank herself into a stupor with her damn Merlot every night. And she was getting fat, looking more and more like her mother every year that passed by. It seemed like every pound she put on put another week between sex for us. Now I'm lucky if it happens five times a year.

It's a relief that at least I've got good genes in that department: even the younger woman at the office still give me the eye. And all the hours at the gym pay off, and started to actually be fun when I started to take Mandy along with me when she got old enough. I will never shit where I eat, but sometimes it is really hard not to imagine getting a little on the side, especially with this younger generation of women who seem to have grown up with no problem at all with sex as fun with no strings: 'hooking up' as they call it.

Thank God that God made us so that our hands reach our groin. He must have known even then that Lisa was going to wind up being one of His creations.

Shit, that's an awful thing to say about anyone, much less your wife! I must really be a bad person. But don't I have a right to my feelings too? Why does everyone else get to be right but I'm always wrong? Except with Mandy, of course .... at least until now.

Christ, she's so petite and still a kid in so many ways, but how many skinny thirteen year-old girls are a C-cup? Every time she got up on my lap her breasts squeezed up against my arm and bounced around in my face when she wanted to play like when she was younger. I felt like total scum for getting affected by it. It's not right, a father having that kind of thing come up around his own daughter. I hate myself for it, truly I do. But with sex with Lisa so rare, am I really such a bad guy? Aren't we men programmed to react this way, slave to our dumbsticks? Even though I would and could never act on it, at least my dumbstick-driven issue is with a female, unlike the damn sodomites in the Church.

What else could I do? I had to stop her climbing up all over me. And I had to stop taking her along on errands and to the gym like I used to because it's too hard to not look at her that way, especially when she dressed in her tight gym clothes. I know it hurt her when I stopped her from getting close any more. But I had to reject her, right? That's the only decent thing a good father could do. Of course I couldn't tell her why, or she'd think there was something wrong with her, when it's what's wrong with me that was the problem.

She'll get over it in time. Kids are resilient: they survive.

But what about me? Since I had to shut her out, I miss our connection so much …. she's so sweet and cute and smart. Christ. It's hard for me to admit it, but Mandy is the kind of girl I always wanted when I was a teenager. It's like God has some sick sense of humor, sending daughters to fathers who then have to deal with them representing their ultimate teenage daydream ideal. How fair is that? How are we supposed to respond? Bad fathers can't control themselves about it and screw up their daughters for a lifetime with their shit. But what are good fathers who are actually honest with themselves supposed to do in a situation like that?

Damn …. i never thought my life would turn out this way.

I'm 36, hate my job even though the pay is great, my marriage is a corpse, my gorgeous daughter will soon start letting other boys paw at her soon, so what's left for me? Maybe I really should check out Alexandra at work. She's only 22 but she's given me all the signals, and my God, what a body on her. It's been so long since I've been with an enthusiastic lover: thirteen years, to be exact. I have never cheated on Lisa. But would it really be bad if it was just something short and intense? Would Lisa really care? Maybe she'd actually be happy about it so she wouldn't have to deal with my frustration all the time about not getting enough sex. God knows I can be an asshole about it.

And don't most shrinks say affairs can be good for a marriage?

Maybe it would give Lisa and me room to fall in love with each other again if I wasn't so frustrated all the time in that department. And maybe if I was more satisfied sexually, I wouldn't be so prone to react to my daughter that way, and Mandy and I could be best friends again, like back in the day.

In that way, maybe it would be a win-win for all of us: me, Lisa, Mandy, and even Alexandra too. Hell, I bet I could take Alex places in bed no kid she's ever been with could. Why didn't I think of it this way before? Wow .... ! Maybe it's time to stop feeling guilty and start living again in ways I've stopped doing!

Alex would have to be discreet, for sure. But I think I can handle her to make sure she went along with the program. Even if word did get around, I'd be the envy of the other guys in the office. We all have that business trip to Dallas next month: perfect!

I wonder if she's really loud when she has an orgasm?

Oh, well. Nothing to do about anything tonight. It's only 7:15, Mandy's in her room doing homework, Lisa's on the phone complaining about her life with her mother, and I've still got two crosswords to do before Stewart comes on .... .

Lucipha-el

As the ang-el-ic ethers pulsed incessantly in their familiar but ever-changing background patterns of energy, emotions, color, and sound, Lucipha-el, sovereign of the Lucipha-el-ite ang-el realm, sat with Ankha-el, his first Advisor, having their annual friendly but intense debate. They had been arguing for a very long time about whether Maker, Source of all things and That Which animates and binds together All That Is, was essentially comprised of Love, Lucipha-el's position, or Will, Ankha-el's view of things.

And also as usual, Micha-el and Gabra-el, sovereigns of the Micha-el-ite and Gabra-el-ite ang-el kingdoms were listening to the conversation via CGS, the Celestial Grid Synaptorium, which allowed ang-els in the three realms to presence with each other from their home realms and so not having to go through the somewhat arduous DRP, or Decompression Recompression Protocol.

DRP was required when ang-els of one realm, being of different energetic and emotive valency than the other two, wished to visit one of the other ang-el realms for wing-to-wing communion, commiseration, and of course, copulangelional activity.

Micha-el-ites were the least energetically dense and valenced with Yin and Love and were most proximal to Maker; the Gabra-el-ites more dense and valenced with Yang and Will, next most proximal; and the Lucipha-el-ite kingdom most energetically dense, with the dominant valences of equal Yin-Yang and Forebearance, or Patience, most distal. The DRP thus made it possible for real-time ang-elic cross-pollination of these different energies and valences and travel through a whole range of domain expressions, allowing commingling of the three different kinds of ang-els, in real Presence.

Only Divine Being in Its Maker Aspect, Parent to all three ang-el domains, knew the algorithms that drove the DRP. The Gabra-el-ites, being of Yang-Will and thus more of mind, had a small but deeply maniacal sub-pod dedicated to decoding the DRP's algorithms as a training to keep themselves sharp in their ongoing soul edgification dynamics. None had yet succeeded, but the work went on. Gabra-el himself headed up the effort, promising one eon soon it would be solved.

After what later would be called one hundred thousand years in something else called time in soul domains not yet formed, all they had succeeded in doing was getting that somehow the DRP wove the threads of Yin, Yang, Mind, Will, Love, and Patience into a living energetic tapestry that could be utilized as a transport mechanism. When they asked Maker for some hints of how this occurred, all they received was Its usual beneficent smile and silent nod, which was Its answer of 'When you figure it out let Me know and we can have some celestea and chat about it.'

The Maker Aspect of Divine Being held the energetic and emotive space for all of Creation and occasionally intervened in long term holding pattern currents in their children's domains, but not in short term ameliorative dynamisms other than nominal maintenance and sustainability effort. It did this so as to allow sentience to both learn on their own to mature, and to provide Itself with insight into some domains of Its actual Nature, which It could only know through the long-term playouts of Its sentient children-species.

"So what's your angle today, Ankha-el?" Lucipha-el asked warmly and pleasantly.

"No need to be so self-satisfied, boss. You might still be wrong," Ankha-el replied.

"There you go again, framing everything in right or wrong rather than true and truer."

"And there you go again, not getting how true and truer can also be expressed and experienced as right or wrong."

"Of course it can. But the danger is that when you cast true and truer into right or wrong energetics, the capacity for trenchant positionality increases exponentially because 'or' always creates content to which one may overattach. But 'and' always creates context, which disallows overattachment."

"As long as you don't always hold contextual perspective, sure. But we ang-els always hold contextual perspective, right?"

"Sometimes I wonder," Lucipha-el replied, narrowing his focus to presence more deeply upon his First Advisor.

The context for the debate was the attempt to really understand the main theme of the Lucipha-el kingdom, which was less clear than the Love of the Micha-el-ites and the Wisdom of the Gabra-el-ites. Everyone agreed it was Forbearance or Patience, but how that Patience actually manifested differed from time to time. It had become clear that if an ang-el lived as if Maker was Will first and Love second, Patience was often much harder to embody. And that if an ang-el lived as if Maker was Love first and Will second, then Patience was more easily embodied.

Of course, one might say more Patience in life was 'better,' implying Maker should thus be seen as Love first. But it was noticed that many times less Patience in any ang-el transaction often created an uncomfortable but ultimately creative tension, out of which an unexpected and more appropriate solution was emergent, one that would never have arisen had more Patience occurred. It was this latter reality that gave Ankha-el the basis for his thesis.

Ankha-el grunted and the game began in the same way it had for millennia.

"Will is the Essence of the Creator, and It expresses Its essential Creative Will-Nature through Love," offered Ankha-el.

"Love is the Essence of the Creator, and It expresses It's essential Love-Nature through Will," replied Lucipha-el.

"All of Creation was brought into being primarily by Will and secondarily held and extended through Love," said Ankha-el.

"All of Creation was brought into being primarily by Love and secondarily held and extended through Will," replied Lucipha-el.

Then Lucipha-el paused to ready himself for any new position to be brought in by Ankha-el. Ankha-el had gathered a significant percentage of Lucipha-el-ites to his camp over the millennia, now nearing thirty percent of the Lucipha-el-ites overall. This was in addition to the almost sixty percent of the Gabra-el-ites, but not Gabra-el himself, and surprisingly, almost five percent of the Micha-el-ites. In that way, Ankha-el had thus amassed just over one-third of all the ang-els to his position.

For the last half-millennia Lucipha-el had sensed a growing anxiety that the issue of this debate had the capacity for some dire consequences, although he could not see what those might be. All of

Creation at the time was the three ang-el realms within Divine Being in Its three aspects of Yang-Maker, Yin-Nonduality, and Child Everything-ness. The Everything-ness domain was represented by all the ang-els of all three kingdoms, children of both the noisy active expressive Maker and the silent still capacitous Nondual. The Micha-el-ites inherited the Yin-Love predominantly, Gabra-el-ites the Yang-Will, and Lucipha-elites the counterintuitive cross-pollinative olio of Yin-Will and Yang-Love aspection.

And since dialogue, debate, and dialectic about the Nature of everything was encouraged by Maker, disagreements were welcomed. As such, Lucipha-el was bothered by his intuition because there was no basis in his reality for it. But something about the one-third percentage of Ankha-el-ian influence bothered him.

As they readied for the next round, an almost silent bass tone rumbled through all three ang-el realms like thunder on an August afternoon, even though neither August nor afternoons had yet been invented. Its specific tonal qualities expressed a call of personal audience to Lucipha-el, asking him to come to the Throne Room for celestea with the Maker.

This was a very unusual event, for even though Micha-el, Gabra-el, and Lucipha-el were in constant countenance with all Aspects of Divine Being, the usual form was one of rapturous ruminative resonance from where they abided in each of their realms. To be called for a Personal Presence Parlay, or PPP, happened only a few times before, after the three sovereign ArchAng-els were given their instructions, and then occasionally for updates and continuing education.

This was before the rest of the ang-els in the three kingdoms had even been created, so this was the first time the three full populations had ever experienced a call to a PPP. To be called on the same day as the much-ballyhooed annual Lucipha-el/Ankha-el debate was even more surprising, because it meant they would have to begin the debate all over again, as protocol required all ang-elic disagreements to adhere to very specific and formal guidelines.

To be called for a PPP meant that neither the CGS nor the DRP would be sufficient. For personal audience with the Maker Itself an ang-el had to undergo Total Etheric Transmutation Protocol, or TERP, to be minimally able to withstand the frequencies of the Maker Domain of Divine Being. TERP left Lucipha-el dizzy for many cycles after he returned to the Lucipha-el realm, but the quantity and quality of energetic residue imparted as a result of presence with Maker was worth it: he could enjoy Copulang-elional Conjugative Connubiality much longer and more deeply after a PPP. This delighted the many Micha-el-ites always ready for CCC with Lucipha-el himself, whose prowess was unmatched in that domain, he of the most dense Yin-Will and Yang-Love dynamisms, and so able to take the Yin-Love based Micha-el-ites to unusually deep depths and high heights of ang-elanimorgasmic intensity, especially after a PPP.

Ankha-el envied Lucipha-el this PPP-mediated prowess, and thought that if he could slowly amass a majority of ang-el to his cause, that he too might one day earn a PPP with the Maker and then also be able to embody a Lucipheric-level CCC with a Micha-el-ite of his choice. Most of the Micha-el-ites did not deign to dance with Ankh-el in CCC, finding him a bit too brutish for their epicurean tastes, elysian sensibilities, and ecumenical ethos. This often left Ankh-el in a frustrated aura, and many of the Lucipha-el-ites apart from his own gang steered clear of him when he went over a millennia without CCC.

As he readied himself for his TERP, Lucipha-el tingled.

What was this about? Maybe some help for how hard it was to hold the overall ang-elic energetic valence of the Lucipha-el-ite realm? Being the most dense ang-el realm of all three, Lucipha-el often struggled to keep the Lucipha-el-ite realm within the confines of the entire ang-el Kingdom, comprised of the two other ang-el realms of much less dense frequencies.

Everyone knew the less dense frequencies of the Micha-el-ite 'pulled' the frequencies 'upward' and proximal toward The Parent, and the more dense frequencies of the Lucipha-el-ite realm 'pulled' the dynamic 'downward' and this distal away from The Parent, with the Gabra-el-ites maintaining ballast between the two. This often caused Lucipha-el himself to strain to keep his, the densest realm, 'buoyed up' enough to maintain inherency within the Ang-elic realm.

Whatever the reason for the PPP, as Lucipha-el prepared himself for Maker interface in real time, a strong shiver moved through him, an unusual vibration that suggested sharpness and weight together. What was that? he wondered. Hopefully not an omen.........

Adam

Sitting had become extremely difficult for Adam in the past six months or so.

He had been working with his Korean Zen teacher for almost seven years, and had been following the dharma religiously as he was taught, that real meditation was never about attaining any particular relaxed, peaceful, or blissful transcendental state. That mistaken goal was what mass consciousness had been taught as the context to do meditation, as just one more element of a still-slave-to-dualism set of modern lifestyle choices.

He had had his fill of westernized consumer-based pseudo-gurus who got rich and famous by teaching people under the aegis of Buddhistic enlightenment how to be happier or more serene, but never led their devotees to the true destination Gotama pointed to, where there was actually no one left at home inside to be happy, unhappy, serene, or conflicted in the first place.

In that way, true enlightenment was only about allowing That Which is beyond all states of mind and consciousness, pleasant or unpleasant, to enter what formerly was your personal state of individualized being, and permanently replace it altogether.

This meant the goal of real enlightenment work could never be taught as attaining any kind of peace, serenity, nonreactivity, bliss, or transformed consciousness that still cycled around a center of self-sentient individual being. Such a distortion could only be mistakenly taught by misguided teachers and accepted by dupable students, those who only wanted amelioration or escape from their worldly troubles, trading one kind of unhappy dualism they wanted to get rid of, for another equally unenlightened dualism of happiness they wanted to cling to.

He had often found it unfathomable how the world could have been so cruelly led so far astray from what Master Gotama originally taught, especially in the west. Only distorted teachings by distorted teachers could explain it. But how to explain how teachers could be so distorted, if they themselves had been taught properly in the proper lineages in the first place? It seemed like there were too few teachers minding the store, as it were, of true Buddhistic dharma and practice. How could this have happened? How did the original teaching of the wholesale replacement of dualistic individualized being by Nonduality devolve in the last few hundred years to a state where an expanded-into-Oneness, and not utterly nullified, dualistic individual being remained, and was thus only dressed up in enlightened clothes and not actually a true embodiment?

Especially appalling to Adam were those who falsely taught the possibility of instant enlightenment or disksha, those who maintained that one could drop their pains and orientations like dropping a coin out of their hand, or worst of all, those who wrote books about Secrets and Powers that only sold concepts and practices of consciousnesses still trapped in states of childish magical thinking. Anyone who bought into that level of nonsense clearly displayed their arrested development. But the tragedy was that they were taught by such authors to believe that it was honest adult spiritual attainment.

He knew that true enlightenment could have no shortcut, and required years of merciless and relentless deconstruction of the very basis of the governing dynamic of personal consciousness. Anything less had to be taught by a teacher who was either woefully misinformed at best, or a fraud at worst. Even though he had compassion for how dupable most seeking people can be, that so many millions bought into these charlatans from the east and west and helped line their pockets was profoundly depressing to Adam. The onus of responsibility had to be with the teachers and their ignorant or intentional misguiding.

In that way, he possessed the true hunger of the real seeker. He had made up his mind that he would accept no teacher whose picture of themselves was on the cover of a book; had a video of themselves teaching on YouTube; had a Facebook or Twitter account; taught to love What Is about everything but then got plastic surgery on their faces; owned their own slick magazines arrogantly maintaining they possessed Absolute Truth; wrote books about conversations with God that said the secret to human life was to just 'let go;' taught how personal will was an illusion, but then were in denial how they used personal will to transcend personal will; sold DVDs of gentle waterfalls and sunsets set to calming new age music but claimed to come from an enlightened perspective; or had appeared as a sanctioned guest or star on mass-consciousness-suffused talk shows that were always looking for ratings, and how that essential motive would never draw a true teacher onto such programs.

Anyone who was thus well-known and popular in the mass culture in any of those ways could only do so from the egos they claimed no longer existed, and had to be selling something that was dumbed-down and so digestible to a popular culture that only wanted to move the content of their beings laterally around a life-chessboard, all the while watching themselves act more enlightened in the mirror of their own ego. The current Dala'i Lama actually taught this was good, that if you just start 'acting' enlightened, which required one to watch themselves in the own mirror of their own ego to do so! How could it be so widely not realized that true enlightenment meant the context of shattering that mirror altogether?

In the end, he decided that any true teacher would never participate in such cultural circus shows or sell true enlightenment short in those ways. A true teacher would more likely be sequestered away in some nondescript monastery somewhere, having no interest in any publicity or wealth, only What Is, and trust anyone meant to learn from them would find them wherever they were.

She or he would probably thus only come out to talk a few times a year for a teaching to their sangha, then return to their quiet lives, and thus never be known to any self-help publishing house looking for profits, or come on the radar screen of talk-shows whose hosts looked to sell their own self-image as a seeker to the masses so as to unconsciously assure it to themselves.

After searching for many years, thinking he would have to trek to Nepal to find such a person, to his utter astonishment Adam had miraculously found just such a one, teaching out of a humble garage in the very city in which he lived. This man was a true rarity, someone who still taught real Buddhistic dharma, that the only real meditation was only and ever about seeking the meditator, and in the end, finding that the meditator could not be found, as the end of all seeking.

In the slow, years-long commitment to the embodiment of that Soto-based meditative realization, aided by an additional track of Rinzai-based radical self-inquiry required to offset the impedimental mental tranquilization risked by too much meditating, one day enlightenment might find the seeker, who realized that they had never existed in the first place in the way they had formerly experienced.

But in the last year of his work, a terror beyond words had started to arise in him. The 'I am' state to which he had moved his 'I' years before, that had at that time resulted in a pervasive universality of porous selfhood that was more at one with everything than in the center of its smaller self, was now slowly approaching what seemed to be an event horizon that could only be described as 'I am not.'

He knew of course that the annihilation of the self and its wholesale and retail perception of itself was the goal of enlightenment effort, but he had not anticipated that an emotion of such magnitude would be part of the process. Most enlightened teachers never spoke of such a deep emotive upwelling, describing the movement instead as one of gentle transcendence resulting one day in a blinding insight out of which the self and all its forms fell away, often accompanied with a burst of freeingly explosive laughter. In that way, it was universally taught that all personally-experienced emotive states were simply other forms of mind-based dualistic arisement, to be watched and transcended in the same ways as thoughts and images.

But in him, that almost existential terror resisted all such effort. The feeling instead was one of slowly dissolving as he bled out the top of his head into a sickeningly horrifying endless whited-out featurelessness. Sometimes it felt as if he was being torn into countless bits of nothingness, at the same time neither his emotive capacity nor his personal center would let go. Strong spasms racked his body at night, interrupting his sleep. His teacher had of course told him that this arising fear was just his ego holding on for dear life and to just keep watching it, that it would dissipate over time as all his thoughts and images always did.

But it didn't: the more he tried to watch the emotion and not indulge in the feeling of it, the more it overwhelmed his watcher-aspect of self. He had been taught in Buddhism, as in Psychology, Science, and Philosophy, that emotions were only a subset of the mind, and could be controlled by the mind in any one of many dozens of ways: attitudinally, pharmacologically, linguistically, or transcendentally. Something about how mind could either control or transcend emotion never sat well with him. But he did know that true enlightenment teaching offered that as the dualistic mind was transcended into That Which precedes it and Of Which the mind cannot touch, so would all powerful emotive states also be automatically transcended.

This occurred because Buddhism specifically taught that emotion was just the part of the mind that over-attached in both attracting and repelling whatever objects his attention focused upon, secondary to the objects themselves. So if all gross and subtle objects of what he called consciousness, including the object of himself, were transcended, so would all the emotional reactivities coiled around them that created emotive-based attraction or repulsion reactions to the objects themselves.

This had worked with all the other less powerful feelings in the past, so it seemed like Buddhism's truth was confirmed. But neither prolonged meditation nor radical self-inquiry seemed to have any affect whatsoever on this deep terror of self-annihilation. In that way, no one had ever told him that any emotion could ever be untranscendable. But that it seemed to be, his teacher had said, only meant that he had to work harder with it.

He thus struggled to keep at it day after day, at one point looking at his meditation bench and seeing it as a seat in a torture chamber, one that he wished he could avoid but would not let himself do so. He watched himself talk to it like it was an enemy of great strength, which did nothing to assuage his anxiety about his state of mind.

So instead of any blissful merging into endless light or relief in the release of the burden of personal self, tidal waves of terror beat relentlessly on him. He wondered what it actually was he was trying to accomplish with all his effort. There was only the torture of annihilation and a sense of the total absurdity of life in itself.

After awhile there didn't seem to be any purpose to making any goal of anything any longer, and without purposefulness, of what use was any effort at all, even the seeking of enlightenment? He had thoughts of suicide, but even that seemed to involve too much investment into what seemed to be useless effort.

It was late in the afternoon that day as Adam was pruning one of his stargazer lily plants. It had rained the night before, and there were still puddles in the gravel paths of the garden. He remembered noting the air was particularly clear and still and that the full moon had begun to rise in the east. He paused a moment to wipe the sweat from his forehead, and noticed that the rising moon was swimming simultaneously in each of three closely aligned puddles in the garden, each reflection of it coming to his eyes from a slightly different angle.

He blinked once and felt a vague stirring. His eyes, what his eyes saw, the puddles, and what the puddles saw as the moon within them were all being pulled together in a curious way. The moment seemed to say a thing's essence could never really be known, only a particular version of it depending on the angle from which it was experienced.

He shook his head to clear his uneasiness.

As his gaze returned to a lily blossom before him, a sudden realization froze Adam to the spot. He was looking directly at the lily, and although he knew the retinas of his eyes were transmitting visual data, he realized in horror he was completely blind, unable to make sense of the flower as a flower. It was as if he'd had a stroke, that the information coming to him from his eyes was being received but not processed. Adam didn't know at the time that all dualistic categories within his consciousness, including the one labeled 'lily,' were washing away. That with the end of those completely artificial compartments came the inability to fit the experience of the lily into any conceptual category in his experience.

He attempted to move from the spot to break the spell, but found he couldn't move a single muscle. Stroke for sure, he thought, convinced each second ticked away the last remaining moments of his life. A sudden panic possessed him but quickly passed, and he found himself accepting his imminent death fully.

How strange, he thought. I'm going to die, and I don't care enough to really be afraid. The entire content of his life summed up as a single, indescribable bubble of sweetness. As it burst in technicolor slow motion, he saw how everything that had ever happened to him was both perfect and perfectly unrepeatable, each moment of it exactly what it should have been, each a completed masterpiece with every color and brushstroke perfectly expressed in shade and composition.

Then suddenly the lily slammed back into his perspective. It burst like fireworks before his eyes, unfolding itself as exploding color and giving him a view of its intricate beauty in such unexpectedly dramatic ways that his eyes brimmed with tears. For the first time in his life Adam experienced the indescribable natural intricacy and beauty of a simple blossom. He was seeing a lily for the first time, the experience of it unfiltered by any compartment within his mind, no dualistic category labeled 'lily' lying between him and his experience of it.

He was only marginally aware of his breath exhaling in wonder. He glanced up inadvertently, and felt his jaw open as the very air surrounding the trees in the garden acquired fullness, as the trees now appeared to be empty vessels penetrating the solid flesh of the air.

In the draw of what seemed to be a last breath, his consciousness attempted to contract as it desperately sought some limit, some defining boundary against which he could lean and rest so as to recover a sense of personalness. That search immediately caused him to slide downward and vaulted him out into a seamless universe lacking any boundary or edge, no matter where he tried to grasp and hold.

Then, in one moment, his eyes, his awareness, the lily, the trees, and the sky came together indivisibly. In that flash, it felt as if he was both rocketed out of the plane of the earth and dropped down a bottomless pit. Adam was only marginally aware he was falling onto the grass. By the time he came to rest on the ground, he was no longer conscious of anything at all.

As he slowly returned to individualized focus, which he felt was about twenty minutes, the lily and the trees and the sky refocused to their former appearance. But they retained an indefinable sweetness linked by a common set of frequency and tones, almost a glow with which only the now-deafening silence within him could resonate.

He reflected mildly about whether the Nondual had finally found him. But that seemed far too onerous a task at the moment, as there was no easy way to summon something else separately out of him to consider anything, no division within that allowed any solid discernment without. He noted that he, whoever that was, was completely indifferent to whether or not any kind of enlightenment had occurred.

In response, he could only smile.

Jeff

The tears flow a little too easily, Jeff thought to himself. They were of course reasonable in one way given how long he'd been with Shari and how much he felt he loved her. But why did it feel like the tears themselves were covering something else? I loved her, truly, he admitted to himself. But she was the one who had left abruptly, saying his love felt like a blanket that kept her skin warm but her insides cold.

How was he supposed to take that?

She didn't even want to talk about it, saying she'd been there, done that. What am I supposed to do, pretend to act ways I know she wants so she feels better? Women .... no matter what man is or tries to be, it's never enough, there's always some kind of shortcoming. Maybe she only felt cold inside because it was she who wouldn't let him get really close, and then blamed him for the effect of her own defenses.

Whatever .... she was gone and his face was wet, but he wasn't in such a bad mood. What do I really feel, he asked himself?

A voice in his head answered evenly: *'You're glad she's gone, and only a baby boy is crying because she's no longer around.'*

The clarity of the words startled him, like someone else with a different voice spoke inside his head. *'Don't be so surprised,'* it replied. *'I am the you you always thought was you, but has never been.'*

Jeff shook his head to try and clear the confusion he felt from this. Am I schizo, he thought? I mean, his Voice Dialogue work had shown him we all have dozens of inner voices at any one time with different pictures of life that had to be heard, accepted, understood, and integrated. But he didn't have to dig for this one, it came to him without effort and was far more definitive than any of the others.

'No, you're not schizo,' the voice said, *'we're both together in this thing you call life. And I'm the one who produces all the other voices to make sure your idiot therapist never finds me, which actually pleases him greatly and makes him think he's effective, because he himself actually doesn't have the actual confidence that he is, codependent as he is with his own wife.'*

"What the hell are you?" he replied, and feeling odd about talking out loud to himself as he moved to the kitchen for a glass of wine. Funny .... what the voice just said about his therapist echoed something he himself had thought at one point, that the subconscious might produce whatever it wants to produce in Voice Dialogue, and that possibility escapes the VD therapist.

'You can call me Cyrano, mate. At your service...!'

Cyrano, huh? Jeff thought. Only a few of his VD voices ever named themselves a human name. There must be a clue about all this in the name, but he couldn't summon up any definite link to a dramatist and thinker from the middle ages, other than remembering de Bergerac was ahead of his time in arguing for reason and trying to ameliorate Christianity with the atomism and ataraxia of the Epicureans.

The familiar sound of the cork popping settled him somewhat as he wondered what to make of the immediacy and power of this inner conversation. The voice was so loud and clear, it really seemed like another person. As a mid-level health insurance manager he was familiar with the standard diagnostic categories of shrinks, but since he knew dissociative identity disorder almost always involved sexual abuse in infancy, he knew for sure he wasn't a candidate, given all the years he had endured working his childhood issues.

Right then the phone rang. It was Shari calling to arrange for her brother to pick up her living room sofa from the flat. "No problem, anytime," he said. "You doing OK?"

"Sorry, no more reasonable concern allowed." she replied. "Heavy blankets can suffocate while they keep you warm," and hung up.

Ouch .... that dig certainly didn't help matters. Metaphors always hurt him the worst, because by the time he digested the power of the statement and realized how deeply it got past his defenses, the time for an equalizing retort was over.

'That's because you give her too much power to hurt you,' replied Cyrano cynically.

Again, so clear, almost shrill: OK, I'll play along, he thought. "But how am I supposed to love a woman if I don't give her the power to hurt me in some ways?" he said out loud.

'By making sure she doesn't have the power to use your love against you,' he replied.

"And how do I do that, my french friend?"

'By never letting her know how much you really do love her, so she is always the yearning one, and in that way off-balance and manageable,' Cyrano said.

Jeff considered this. Wherever Cyrano came from, he wasn't stupid. "Only a manipulative and controlling macho asshole would say such a thing."

'And the problem is …. ?'

"The problem is all that patriarchal crap is just an insecure frightened little boy acting out to protect himself from his terror of women," Jeff replied.

'Precisely. You are the insecure frightened little boy and I am your compensation, you the little boy who loved Shari like a warm blanket and I the compensation to make sure her insides were left cold so she wouldn't get so close. You think your insight about macho assholes means we are not one, which amuses me greatly.'

Jeff's mouth opened in astonishment. Could this conversation be the result of that bad mushroom trip in my twenties? But what it had just said was a really clear insight that was off my conscious radar…..what in hell is going on here? Since when do inner voices just come and confront you with insights like that?

'Relax, pal. She had her own matriarch and amazon running that I had to rise to fight. We're better off without her in the long run,' Cyrano offered.

This is nuts, he thought, as he reached for the bottle.

'That's it, brood boy: go to the teat of the grape-mama, who will take you to dreamland and smooth away all the hard edges.'

"Hey, I'm a happy drunk, OK? Everybody loves a happy drunk."

'Sure you are, and yes they do,' Cyrano relied. *'But happy drunks are really sad way deep down, just like belligerent ones are scared way deep down. So be happy that you're sad, go ahead. And if that doesn't work, you can always go back to the tobacco-mama you used when you were younger. She was made specifically to hook you by matching the shape of mama's nipple, has nicotine to calm the anxiety, and engineered for delivery by taking advantage of the unconscious infantile suck reflex! It's so funny to watch people think they are sophisticated and grown up when they smoke, when all they are doing is displaying to the whole world that they still need mommy like babies to feel safe and comforted by the breast.'*

"Are you supporting me or criticizing me?" Jeff said with an edge as he poured a full glass of his favorite pinot gris. *What the hell, if I'm talking to myself already I might as well drink.*

'Why, supporting you of course. The more you sip, suck, or simper, the less hard I have to work making sure you don't actually feel emotion.'

"So that's your job, to not let me feel what you don't want to feel?"

'No, brood boy.....my job is to make sure you don't feel what you don't want to feel, but think you do,' he said.

"What do you mean?"

'You think you want to feel, but you don't. If you really knew what it was to actually feel all the way down to your core, you would run like the wind in the other direction, and make sure your mind never let them come up, and your behaviors were intense enough to distract you..'

"Hey, I'm a guy, right? Feeling feelings is for therapy, not real life. The only feelings we're supposed to have in real life are the ones women want us to have, the ones we need to give them so then we can get what we want in the other way, right?" he said, winking.

Cyrano seemed to smile. *'Now you're starting to get it, grape-boy. But not quite: you need to only give women the feelings that you think that they think they want.'*

Jeff considered this. *Maybe this voice wasn't so bad. He was on my side after all, supporting me being in charge of things. I'm pretty intuitive in knowing what women think they want. I can work with that,* he thought, *no problem.*

'Sure you can, pal. Check with me in a pinch: I'll always steer you away from whatever might make you feel too uncomfortable. All I ask in return is that you keep sipping, sucking, or simpering to make it easier for me to help you. If we stick together and neither of us try to hog all the life-space, we can get what we want with a minimum of risk.'

"I can live with that," Jeff thought to himself. He raised his glass and said, "Cheers ....!" but without a smile. "To the grape-mama in all of her forms!" as he began to drink hungrily.

'Yeah yeah yeah,' Cyrano said to himself, without letting Jeff hear him. *'Christ. The things I have to go through to make sure he stays out of trouble. God, that wine tastes so frigging bad! I wish he liked vodka better. I could really rest with that stuff, it would keep the inner kids quiet better. Now...where was I? Oh, yeah, thinking about Clarisse at Jeff's work. If I can*

find out what she drinks for afternoon coffee, I could bring it to her as a surprise. That'll get her thinking Jeff's a different kind of guy than what she's used to. Then I'll tell her I can't decide if my favorite movie is Titanic or The Notebook, and with both she'll spread her legs for sure.'

He relaxed into that thought. *'OK,'* he said to himself. *' I can still make Jeff think he's in charge even though I had to show myself. Now, how to make sure his damned therapist never has a clue about what I'm up to. I can always float another three or four voices, that'll throw him off the trail for sure. Things are looking up .... .'*

She

And there was she, embers still glowing
beneath the damp wood of yesterday's fire
her heart over-worn from too many days of night,
a desert flower refusing to accept its day in the sun has passed

her heart hungry for the sound of its own color
an overgrown trail in a forest of forgetfulness
eyes finding only unspoken tongues of felt pasts
in a mosaic with a shard of purple missing

there, a memory floats on liquid green clouds too far afar
in thirst for a torrent of a perilous private passion
carved from the dry clay of a riverbed unquenched
by the spring-waters of a necessary solace

make me hear raindrops, she dreamed, that i feel my life
their pale color made bright by shimmering shadows
too long my moments have rung hollow by overworked words
and sung from the voice of lilacs not yet bloomed

my tears mix uneasily with the smile of angels
and my breath moves in a gale of shattered glass
sighing, as the path woven before my birth
is planted like moonlight on water yet unseen by stars

Giles & Katherine

"Good morning and welcome to Coupling and Co-parenting, a one-day seminar to introduce you to a unique new way of looking at intimate relationship and its link to heart-felt parenting. I'm Giles Bishop, and this is my wife Katherine Bingham Bishop." Katherine nodded to the audience. "We also have two children, Analee and Christopher, who decided the latest version of Halo was more interesting than coming to hear mom and dad talk about boring things like parenting and relationships."

The audience chuckled.

Katherine offered, "So we're here to basically address questions and concerns about the themes that govern our picture of coupling and co-parenting. We presume all of you have read the basic handbook or you wouldn't be here, so we're to discuss any issue that the handbook may have brought up in you, pro or con."

"Con is the applicable word," said a late-thirty-ish man in the front row. "This whole thing is a con job from the get-go."

"Can we have your name, please?" asked Giles.

"Peter will do."

"Okay Peter, will you please tell us what you find disagreeable?" Katherine replied.

"The question is, do I find anything agreeable? Because what this handbook says is that the way we have been looking at both romantic relationship and parenting has been wrong all along. Is there no limit to your arrogance?"

Katherine responded, "That is fundamentally correct, in that what we are saying does counter almost one hundred and fifty years of psychological and philosophical guidance in this domain."

"And five thousand years of religious opinion," added Giles.

Katherine nodded and continued, "But arrogance is only a secondary way to relate to any kind of held truth. We hold our truth, but don't claim it is any kind of absolute, that no human being, no matter how enlightened, can ever know or represent any Absolute, and those who claim they can, have serious megalomaniacal narcissistic issues. That means we're not arrogant, as it would only be arrogance if we thought our truth was an absolute."

"Yes," said Giles. "This especially applies to religions and enlightened teachers, the ones who most often claim possession of Absolute Truth. The egotistic narcissism involved in such a position is itself the compensation for claiming to either see ego as inherently bad or claim to have no ego at all. In our picture it is impossible for anyone to not have an ego or that ego is inherently bad. The issue is, is the ego emotionally mature or emotionally immature? Only an immature ego attaches and repels; a mature ego does neither."

Katherine interrupted, "We don't want to get ahead of ourselves here. We'll talk more this afternoon about the spiritual ramifications of our picture. For now, Peter, it's not arrogant at all to offer what we do, any more than it is arrogance for someone to simply disagree with the status quo. Or how it wasn't arrogant for Copernicus or Galileo to counter the geocentric view of the universe in their day. New shifts in the way of looking at things are almost always seen as heretical when they're first introduced."

"Your metaphor implies you think your picture will be vindicated as the only truth one day, proving then that you were right and that we were all wrong about our opinions. Do you deny that?" Peter replied strongly.

"Not at all," Katherine responded gently. "We really do think what we teach will one day be seen as more inclusive and more wisely applicable to human beings than current opinions in this area by religion, philosophy, anthropology, and psychology. Evolution of consciousness goes on, new things replace old ways of looking at things .... what do you find upsetting about that?"

Peter ignored the question, pointed to a page in the handbook and said, "It says here every couple is naturally immature until they do deep emotional work in your specific way, and that all parenting is naturally harmful to children unless the parents have done your work," Peter replied.

"That's right," said Giles warmly. "But only because the vision that governs why we say and do what we say and do is not offered anywhere else for the moment. What about that bothers you?"

"What bothers me?' Are you crazy? You are accusing all parents of consciously abusing their children unless they do it your way!"

"Peter, we are not," said Katherine. "They don't consciously do it. How could parents do anything different than what our conditioning, our cultures, and our experts have taught us so far? What we're saying is that the religious, spiritual, psychological, and philosophical paradigms that have been guiding us about what a human being is, what children actually need in childhood, how parenting needs to provide those needs, what constitutes emotionally mature couplehood, and the place emotions have in our lives, have never been clear enough in the past to help us do mature relating with partners, peers, or kids."

Giles smiled kindly and added, "Wait....let's put content aside for a moment and look at the context. Peter, it's obvious you've already made up your mind that you disagree with our picture. If our particular shoe doesn't fit you, why are you wearing it long enough to be made so upset about it? Why did you come at all after reading the handbook? Why not just trust yourself enough to say 'these people are crazy,' throw away the book, and not waste time here because you don't agree with it?"

"Because what you people peddle is dangerous!"

"To whom?" Giles replied.

"To, to .... to anyone who gets near it!" Peter cried.

Giles nodded. "We would unapologetically say that it is indeed dangerous to people's defenses and conditioned patterns," Giles replied, with no hint of condescension. "But that means that if someone feels it is dangerous, only their defenses and fear would react that way. Non-defensivity would either want to know more on the one side, or simply shrug and walk away in disagreement on the other."

"Bullshit! People will get duped into it and then their lives will fall apart! I know! I have talked to some people who worked this stuff and left it! They confirm it ruined their lives! You are a cult! Someone needs to stop it!"

"Peter, do you think it's possible maybe those people did as much as they could with what we offer, but then hit some internal defensive wall and that their fear got triggered later than sooner, which then came out as negative reactivity?" Katherine replied kindly, with no critical tones. "Maybe what they say got ruined is only a narrower or more unconsciously fear-based way of living that the conscious personality initially came to this work to change, but then a wounded part of them desperately wanted to hold onto."

Peter, getting heated up, said, "Don't twist what I am saying! I am saying that your way of looking at romance and parenting will make people lose every .... ."

"Hey pal, give it a rest, OK? said another man in the audience. 'Methinks you protesteth too much.' "Maybe what they say here makes you so uncomfortable you have to fight it to defend your own world in some way, and that would mean you're just threatened by it or afraid of change."

"Yes," said the woman next to him. "If you've decided you don't like it, that's cool, no one's holding a gun to your head, but then just leave, OK? Some of us want to hear more about this. If you have to fight something the way you are fighting right now, you're in denial that it actually applies to you and you don't want to face into that. And I don't need you or anyone else to tell me what is dangerous or not or to protect me from anything."

Giles sighed. Not even five minutes and we're already deep in it, he thought. Will this kind of projection thing ever end? Is our species somehow so insecure and entrenched they have to resist anything that threatens conditioned patterns?

"Wait, please," replied Katherine. "Maybe all Peter has to do is clear this up front and then we can get onto more content that may address what he finds troubling. Does that work for you, Peter?"

Another young woman stood up shouting, "I agree with Peter. What you want is the destruction of the family as we know it!"

"In one way, that's exactly right," Giles replied warmly. "We can demonstrate how the average couple and family dynamics as we have been globally conditioned to create are almost wholly dysfunctional, and not seen as such because the dysfunctionality is so universally normalized we can't see it. We actually believe in the family so much we want to help family systems become healthier and move past the dystrophic family 'as we know it' to couple and family dynamisms that are more emotionally mature instead. But we do not hold that as 'destruction.' We hold it as 'healthy change.'"

The woman opened her mouth to say something, but nothing came out. Peter had told her these people hated the family, which made them evil. She wasn't prepared to find them so reasonable.

Peter noticed her confusion and stood up. "Never mind, fine. I'm leaving, but you can be sure my blog 'Cults and Dolts' will expose what you are teaching here as dangerous. Read it and weep." He turned to the audience. "All of you are sheep who are so weak you need a shepherd to lead you because you're so lost. Only those shepherds are wolves," Peter said, pointing to Giles and Katherine.

Many people in the audience laughed, some kindly, some unkindly. With that, Peter stalked out of the room, and three other people followed him.

"Guess he has some authority issues, huh?" said the older woman who spoke earlier. "He obviously came pre-loaded and had no interest in knowing why his reaction was so big. People like that are never interested in examining the 'why' of their big reactions: they think because they have them so strong they must be 'right.' How can they not get that a big reaction always means, 'I can't look at this because it threatens my value system.' Looks like daddy or mommy never gave him any room for his own reality, so he's stuck in a teenage arrested development stage of rebellion-against-authority. That's really sad."

"Very incisive," Giles noted. "And I'm so glad you said 'sad.' People like Peter are hurting, and should never be objects of derision. Are you a therapist of some kind, and can we have your name please?"

"Janine Powell, and yes, I'm a Jungian analyst. "I'm so impressed neither of you got hooked into reacting to him the way he did with you, at the same time you didn't pull back your empathy to do that. That's rare to find in teachers because you can't fake that. Most teachers who don't get triggered by people like Peter are either transcending or above it all, know what I mean? They don't connect anyway. But you didn't: you stayed with him with acceptance and warmth while he bashed you. Does your emotional work help you do that? You didn't seem to be controlling down anything."

"Well if you mean, does it allow us to hold our centers without losing either emotive immediacy or energetic porosity, then yes," Katherine replied. "Our work specifically allows such an embodiment of that kind of personal strength and vulnerability, with no controlling of anything. My heart always aches for people like Peter, we see them a lot, either up front like here, or halfway into their journey, when so often at that stage a line gets drawn by the defenses and cries victim."

Giles added, "Only people who have huge defenses get triggered like Peter and have to leave in a huff earlier or later, vowing vengeance. People who don't, don't. The bigger the victimized negative reaction, the bigger the defenses."

Katherine sighed, honestly and without any superiority energy. "Yes .... and that level of defense is always equal to the level of unconscious unhealed woundedness underneath which it protects: you wouldn't need a defense otherwise. The blogs are full of hurt people like Peter, where they can get their defenses digitally co-signed by others in cyberspace with similar woundings, as a way to not deal with the deeper issues that drive the victimhood, consoling each other about the big bad wolves or cults they think have abused them."

"But don't most cults actually harm people?" another man in the audience asked.

"Of course," Katherine replied. "Groups led by horribly wounded leaders covering up their issues with spiritualized claptrap harm people every day. But only to the degree the adults let them, right? In such a case of voluntary participation, who makes them do what the leaders tell them to do? If adults let a group abuse them, don't they have to take responsibility to look at why as grown-ups they let themselves get abused? If they did, they would never cry victim or react so deeply, because they'd know they co-created what they experienced by choosing to be part of it in the first place."

"Exactly right!" said Janine. "It's so good to hear someone else say this! Almost all cult de-programmers frame such situations that people are poor-baby victims of the bad leaders. I know, I've done that kind of work but left it for that reason. Most de-progammers co-sign the victimhood of the people they help without ever holding them responsible, and that keeps them stuck in child stages of development.'

She added passionately, "Internet cult-alerters and most de-programmers may care about people, but they never worked their own issues of abuse from childhood authorities, and use their role helping others to never deal with that. Like the poor-me victim devotees on the other side of the coin, they become the saviors of the victimized, project their own mommy and daddy issues onto new authority figures, fight them, and think they are 'freer' because of it, when all they're doing is shadow-boxing with their own issues, literally."

Giles shook his head. "Do you know how rare it is for us to find people like you who get that? In this age where everyone's a victim in cyberspace and so few take the responsibility for their own choices in their half of any transaction?"

"We hold the only true victims in life are children, because they can't choose their way out of dystrophic households. Seen that way, the only real cult is the family, in the sense that the family is where impressionable children are helplessly conditioned to process reality very specifically in ways that have to be unraveled later to ever find their own truths. Some families are better cults and some are worse, but a cult is only really definable as such if it contains children who can't choose out of it. To say an adult is part of a cult is ridiculous, because they can always choose out."

"But what about people who are brainwashed into thinking they can't leave?" asked the same man who asked before.

"Then those people have to ask themselves why they were so broken and wounded by their own childhood that they were brainwashable in the first place," said Katherine. "Either way, they are not victims of the cult leaders they project they are, they are unhealed victims of their own cult-family-of-origin that helped create a being with so little healthy center they were either brainwashable or controllable. In that way, we have unlimited heart-space for the inner wounded being of an ex-cult person, but no space whatsoever for the part of them that covers that with 'I am a victim!' Supporting the victim part actually prevents the inner wounded part from ever getting the help they really need."

Giles nodded and said, "Adults like Peter who feel they must fight against something like what we do, instead of just disagreeing, really believe they are not being victims because they fight. Almost no one realizes that fighting itself can only be done if you already feel like a victim. It's heartbreaking how many good people tragically display arrested emotional development to that degree in that way. While they flail against their imaginary devils, the underlying wounds that drive the flailing are locked out of ever being confronted and healed."

"In those ways, Peter is trying to 'save' others from our 'evil' as an unconscious way to try and save a part of himself who was victimized in childhood by his original authority figures in some way. While he does that, the little Peter inside him goes unnoticed, unloved, and un-healed. And the family values conditioning we get imprinted by is based so deeply in outworn religious ethics. It is exactly the bad soil that produces the rotten fruit of our expressed forms of families as we know them, that all pass as normal. "And you sir?" he added, re-ferring to the man who spoke first.

"Zack Powell. I'm with her," he said pointing to Janine, smiling. "I'm a teacher and counselor in a residential high school for troubled teens, and I know a victim projecting perpetration on someone as an unconscious stand-in for his own parents, all the while inside his own closed universe, when I see one."

"Wow .... again a really clear understanding," Katherine said. "You two have obviously done a whole lot of work." Giles nodded.

"Hell yes," Zack replied. "Over twenty years of it. But something was always missing in all the otherwise good things Janine and I ex-plored. We couldn't put our finger on it, but when we read your hand-book, something clicked. How parents of the last generation who listened to the experts who said they should always say 'yes' to their kids have damaged them just as much as the parents who always en-ergized the 'no?' Incredible! And how couples who never mature themselves emotionally before relationship are codependent, no mat-ter how well they communicate, behave, or otherwise think they are loving each other?"

"We'll get into more of that shortly," said Katherine.

Another man in the audience raised his hand and said to Giles, "Are you saying we should never fight against any injustice because that would show you are a victim?"

Giles answered, "What's your name, please?"

"Nathan."

"Nathan, no, of course not. Where would we be if non-whites hadn't fought against racial discrimination in this country, or if woman didn't fight against being raped, or if women hadn't fought against the patriarchy and all of its effects?" Giles said.

"Or if people wanting to be more individually free hadn't fought against either fascistic or socialistic collectivism and dictatorships of all kinds?" Katherine added.

Giles nodded and continued, "As Katherine just said, it's a case of 'voluntary in, voluntary out,' or 'involuntary in, fight your way out.' We must fight when cultural systems, governmental fiat, or corporate greed abuse those whom they serve in situations where people didn't fully choose their way into the situation in which they have been wronged or served unjustly. In that way, you don't voluntarily choose into governmental abuse, general societal oppression, being robbed, patriarchal abasement, police brutality, or irresponsibly handled corporate pollution of drinking water. People didn't directly voluntarily choose into those situations, so they have to fight their way out."

"But when an adult consciously and voluntarily chooses into something they don't have to be part of in any way, like a group, cult, psychospiritual transformative path, or religion, if they find out after going into it that it wasn't what they thought, since they had the freedom to choose in, they have the freedom to choose out, to leave at any time. As such, they only play victim to their own choices like a child when they cry they have been abused or not well-treated by the cult, path of work, or religion they chose to be part of as an adult in the first place."

"Yes," said Katherine. "A grown-up adult who feels that what they got themselves into was not good, would just walk away and ask themselves 'what unconscious wound in me caused me to not see the badness ahead of time?' and emporingly get into some kind of therapy to try to learn why they gave up their self-sovereignty so readily. When they do that, they take responsibility for their initial choice and so never abdicate self-responsibility by crying 'I was victimized by them! They are evil!"

"In our picture," Giles concluded, "if someone hits me in the head with a club, I don't cry, 'I am a victim!' even though that is exactly what our cultures and families condition into us. I ask myself, 'why didn't I see it coming?' We hold this is actually what Jesus meant when he said, 'Turn the other cheek': not to be a powerless enabler of someone doing harm to you, as most think it means, but to take responsibility for your half of all co-created experience with others. If you did, you would never feel victimized, ever. If Christianity ever got that one point right, which they never have, their religion would become so different it would be unrecognizable. Does that help?"

"It does, thank you," said Nathan.

Giles added, "Many pseudo-spiritual teachers eschew any form of tough love, believing that, as in this case, the not supporting of victimhood is wrong. But since everyone is wounded from childhood, everyone has defenses, and everyone has some defenses that run self-justifying victim scenarios as a strategy to continue to blame some outside agent as a projection of their own parents for their pain, so they can siphon some of it off that way."

He sighed deeply. "The victim behaviors, and everyone has them to some greater or lesser degree, have to be tough-loved inside a greater vision of supporting the person's true bigness and potential. Victimhood embodiment is as pervasive and poisonous a drug as alcohol or drug abuse. Not confronting victimhood in the same way you'd confront abuse of drugs or alcohol with tough love means enabling the defense and helping a person stay a child."

"If that's true, then why didn't you confront Peter in a tough love way?" asked Zack.

"Because he didn't give us permission to bring that level of response to him, which is only done when someone decides to explore what we do. People who do, specifically ask us to reflect what we see that their own insulative defenses may not let them see about themselves: they want to know, even if it is not pleasant, and much of it is not. Only then is there a mutually agreed-upon covenant of work that might on occasion include tough love, which Peter had not agreed to. In that case, it would be abusive and not right to bring it him. Does that make sense?"

"It does, thanks," replied Zack. "Very cool."

"You have more respect for him than he did for you," Janine said.

"How else can we bring what we feel with integrity?" Giles replied. "It is actually truer to say in that sense we had more respect for him than he did for himself."

"Yes!" said Zack. "How so few people ever get that!"

Giles continued, with increasing intensity. "Teachers or therapists who decry tough love only broadcast their own unhealed issues about never being loved enough in their own childhoods, so they coddle those with whom they work as a way to unconsciously caretake their own unconscious woundings. You could say that if a helper really did love people, they would always be ready to confront, both with love and strength, what may be uncomfortable for the helpee, in order to help the person attain what they came to them for in the first place, their own greater and healthier being."

"And that if they don't do this, those kind of non-tough love helpers don't really love people in any personal way, which of course is true for spiritual teachers, who by and large only love people universally or unconditionally, and in not personal frequencies of love. Universal or unconditional frequencies of love only give a person a refreshing impersonal universalized bath when they feel dirty, and not the personal water to drink that they actually need as they are dying of thirst, which can only be delivered up close in personal and not universal relational spaces."

"This is also why enlightened Buddhist teachers can't ever really help anyone, because in their picture there is no real thing called the personal in the first place. They may inspire, but the content of their inspiration only takes people out of suffering by taking them out of the personal, which never heals anything, only covers the suffering with transcendental process, just another drug, albeit a more sophisticated one. Impersonal universal- or unconditional-based teachings can inspire, but only personal-based teachings can help us really change anything. For us, inspiration without imparting real change is impotent, and needs to be recognized as such."

Giles realized then he'd been tirading, and stopped himself. "Sorry," he said, a bit sheepishly. "If you work with people and really care about them as long as I have, you get pretty passionate about how little gurus and therapists serve people, they who think they help others change without ever knowing that real change is about being emotionally mature in the domain of the personal."

Katherine added, "The personal domain has to be authenticated emotively and seen as spiritually real, not processed as a pass-through as a way to realize it is nothing in its essence, as Buddhism teaches. Other questions?'

A woman in the back stood up. "My name is Renee. Can you please explain why you say in the handbook that a child raised with the heart-food they actually needed when they were young, would never become a rebellious teenager?"

"Yes," she replied. "If a child does not adequately get fed the appropriate heart-food they need in their emotional body as young children, the essence of which we have never been taught in any of our guiding paradigms of child development or parenting process, when they get to be a teen and begin to assert their appropriate independent aspects, they find they then have the power to finally resist the parents who never provided that heart-food, even though they don't know that is why they are acting out. If they do get fed that food for their emotional bodies, there's no unconscious need to make the parents' pay and so there is no need to express acting-out behaviors."

Renee replied, "So even if parents really love their kids, that doesn't qualify as the adequate heart-food for them in your picture? That seems unbelievable."

"It did to me too when I first encountered this way of looking at things," Giles responded. "I have learned and have had it experientially verified with our own kids that a child's emotional body has only one need: real heart-food for a child is having the experience that parents feel what the child is feeling while the child is feeling it. Having that experience is the only basic form of 'love' a child needs, in that sense. If that is provided, everything else will fall into place, and if it is not, nothing else will make up for its lack. To actually be able to do that requires parents to be something none of us are naturally, conditioned as we have been by our world. Parents would need to be emotively and energetically opened up, which no one can while still carrying their own unconscious emotional body deficits from their own family-of-origin."

He sighed and continued, "Parents can really love their kids, but when they feel love for them or pour love on them from behind an unconscious emoto-energetic barrier in their heart-fields that neither they, psychology nor psychiatry can see or track, the love does not cross the relational space to the child, who does not have the experience of feeling parents feel what they are feeling while they are feeling it, and so are left unfed."

Katherine added, "That old kind of parenting might physically deposit a 'normal,' societally-functional child at the doorstep of adulthood, but that 'normal' societally-functional person is an emotionally dystrophic adult who is an amalgam of strategies, inauthenticities, unhealed wounds and resentments, and triggerable for projections. As such, they are not equipped to live an 'abnormal,' supple, internally healthy, and joyful life, where a deep and abiding thrival, and not just functional survival, is possible in any deep or real way."

"So that's why the handbook says real parenting is not about what you do, but who you are," Renee replied.

"Yes, exactly," Katherine said. "A real parent is someone who has become the kind of person who both role-models emotional maturity to children and, even when they make mistakes, engenders self-love and self-responsibility in their kids because they raise them to be whole and authentic, and not fractionated or strategic. Real parenting requires parents to become a very different kind of person before having children than what our cultures, families, and religions teach us to be. And that requires us to do a huge amount of work on ourselves to be that more authentic version of ourselves before we ever become parents. If we don't, we will pass the emotional body 'gene' of familial dystrophy by default down to yet another generation, as it has been over and over for thousands of years."

Janine asked, "What do you mean when you say in the handbook about how all the hidden damage done to children by even well-meaning parents who love their kids is caused by counter-transference from parent to child?"

"That's a big topic we'll go more into this afternoon. For now, we can say that unless parents self-authenticate and become emotively mature before having children, they will inevitably either be emotively and energetically too close to their kids, creating gross or subtle abuse, or emotively and energetically too far from their kids, creating gross or subtle neglect. This means, in the absence of embodying emotional maturity before having kids, parents will inevitably need their own children to meet their own unmet emotive needs from their own childhood in some way. That is the counter-transference."

"Healthy parents need nothing emotively from their children: nothing. To the degree they do need something emotively from their children, and they will in the absence of emotional maturity, because they never healed their own family-of-origin issues, they will either feed off their children, try to live through them, or distance themselves from them because they trigger too many unconscious unhealed issues from their own childhood."

"So any child who feels they have some duty to serve the emotional needs of a parent as they get older has only been conditioned to do so by an emotionally dystrophic parent, and to that degree, the child never has the room to have their own emotional needs met as they become parent to the parents. Voila, emotionally dystrophic children who will do the same to their children, and then their children to theirs, on and on."

Katherine took a breath and passionately said, "Being conditioned to serve the emotional needs of parents, which almost all of our cultures see as appropriate, collapses the holding space the child needs the parent to provide for them so that they can get their own needs met. That almost all of that counter-transference resulting in either abuse or neglect is unconscious to parents, neither absolves them of responsibility of what they are doing nor lessens the damage they do to their children as a result."

Another man stood and asked, "I'm Alan. So you're saying adult children should never serve the needs of frail parents as they age?"

Giles shook his head. "No, no, not at all. That's a physical domain, not necessarily an emotional one. What we are saying is that there should be no emotively compulsive guilt-driven motive to help, such that if they don't do it, they are bad and fail their parents: that would be the abusive emotional blackmail the parents imprinted into them in childhood. An adult child can certainly choose to help older parents in ways that do not sell out their own truths, but that choice needs to be non-guilt-driven. Compulsive, guilt-driven motives to help anyone actually never come from the heart! When people do come from guilt-driven motives, there are always unconscious resentments going on underneath, which means it can't come clean from the heart. Does that answer your question?"

"Yes, it does, thank you," said Alan.

Katherine continued, "So those deficits from childhood held that way in the child's emotional body remain throughout life," Giles added. "So when they grow up and begin having intimate relationships, those unmet needs or deficits that should have been provided by parents are then unconsciously sought to be fulfilled by their adult partner to some significant degree, creating rabid codependence. Because the seeking of those unmet needs from childhood from the adult intimate partner is so unconscious, and is also not tracked well enough by psychology, psychiatry, or spiritual paradigms that do not see the emotional body as primary to the mental body, the degree of codependence created by that projective need is also not tracked. In that way, no one is qualified to have children who hasn't yet completed their own childhood before they do!"

"The process we offer, which takes four to five years to minimally complete, allows people to finally complete their childhoods energetically and emotively so their past no longer lives in their future. Only then are they minimally capable of noncodependent romance and non-counter-transferential child-rearing. In the end, it's that simple and that hard."

Zack said, "Yikes. If all of that's true, that really would change everything we thought we knew about romance and parenting."

"And the true nature of self-esteem," added Janine.

"It would," replied Giles," if what we are saying is true. But since we just hold it as our picture and not as any absolute, as well as being completely verifiable to anyone willing to test it over time, let's talk more about why the human emotional body and its primacy over the mental and physical bodies has never been seen by any secular, religious, or spiritual paradigm in history........"

Three days after the seminar ended, Peter was writing in his blog Cults and Dolts. *'Well folks, we have another cult for you to be on the lookout for. This one is about brainwashing people that the mind can never control emotion, despite what all the real experts say. And because it can't, that means everything we have been taught about parenting and romantic relationship is wrong, and so only their picture is the right and absolute truth. They also say all spiritual teachers who give people unconditional and universal love are wrong! I guess Jesus and the Buddha are bad guys to them!*

Keep your adult kids and your significant others away from this one, and warn your friends and family how dangerous it would be to get involved with them: it would mean your whole life would collapse around you. If you're interested in picketing their next seminar in your hometown, send me an email and we'll make sure you can be part of fighting this arrogant

group dead set on the destruction of the family and all the right values we
live by that are true and.....'

"Peter Knowles!" his mother called from the kitchen upstairs, down to the basement of her house, where he'd lived for the last seven months since his wife left him. "Get up here and clean up this mess you left right now!"

"Yeah, yeah, yeah," he said under his breath so she couldn't hear. "I'd like to tell you where to stick that mess, you old bag. You're just like Beth was, always ragging on me, nag, nag, nag. Women need to get a life and stop telling their men what to do .... ."

Lisa

Lisa shuffled from the kitchen to the living room and plopped heavily down on the Lazy-Boy, the coffee in her hand barely not spilling over. Another blank day ahead. Mandy's at school, Larry's gone to work, the cat's been fed, and the day yawned open in front of her. I used to write poetry all the time, she thought. It was pretty good, too. I can barely remember the me who did that. Where did she go? Who is this person sitting here wishing something would save her from herself and her life?

I know I have it better than most people, with a husband who provides a good living, a smart beautiful kid who's healthy and popular at school, and the gift of not having to work to keep the household in money. Sure, I've gained a few pounds, but who at 35 looks like they did at 18? All in all, it isn't so much that things in my life are bad as much as they are just so .... bland.

I think Larry has been screwing that Alex bitch at work for awhile now, she thought. He hasn't been bothering me much for sex for over a year, and that's unusual for him. How do I feel about that? Mixed, she decided. It made her want to kill him in one way but there was some relief in another, but not because she didn't like sex, because Larry was great in bed. It was because she then didn't have to worry so much about the herpes thing, the scarlet letter of her world, her worst and best-kept secret pain and guilt.

She had never told Larry that she had gotten herpes from her high school boyfriend Martin about a year before she had met him. When she had found out he himself had gotten it from her best friend Connie, she was crushed beyond words. She had to end connection with the two closest people in her life at the same time, the hardest thing she had ever done.

That left no one but her mother and father for consolation, and obviously all they could do was spout their usual Catholic litany with Jesus talking about forgiving one's enemy, the sin of lust, God's response to Sodom and Gomorrah, yadda-yadda. Then when she met Larry, and he was so good-looking, sensitive for a guy, and was so attracted to her, it seemed like he was her reward for being screwed so badly by her ex-friend and ex-lover.

She resolved to tell him about the herpes the closer they got to doing sex, but she was terrified a really great guy like him would drop her like a rock if he found out. At the time, she had had only three outbreaks before meeting him, the initial one and two repeats, and it always let her know way ahead of time it was coming before she started shedding virus. She thought that if she was vigilant, she could arrange their sex life around it for awhile, and would eventually tell him about it later if they stayed together and things got more serious.

But then she got pregnant with Mandy after only about four months with him, and everything was hell again, even worse. No way could she get an abortion with her parents still supporting her with everything, car, apartment, money. Their whole life would become a gossip item for the small Catholic community they lived in. She thought her mother would have a stroke when she told her, because she actually fainted when she did, and her father screamed at her for being a whore and that this was God's punishment for her filth.

That frightened her horribly, because even though she quietly rejected most of their fervent beliefs, she also still had a semblance of her own lifelong Catholic conditioning about fear of an angry God's retribution for sin. The nun she had in the sixth grade had actually told her class that God hated all women so much for how it was Eve who made Adam sin in the Garden of Eden, that He had cursed women forever with the painful monthly flow because of it. Even though her adult mind now saw that as laughable and horrifically patriarchal bullshit, some remnant of that still registered like a thorn somewhere in her.

Goddam those nuns. Dried up hags, most of them. The one or two she'd known who were sweet and loving never made a dent in the majority of masculinized horrors she had to endure in one of the last Catholic grade schools in the country that still had all nuns teaching every grade and subject. How could a de-feminized virgin covering her unconscious issues with piety teach girls about what it was like to be a woman in regular life?

She remembered that Larry was completely shocked about the pregnancy because they were really careful with condoms, and she always used foam. She couldn't do the pill, because it made her so fat so fast. At first she thought he was going to run, but then something changed in him and he took a step and got closer instead. When he asked her to marry him a few weeks later, she thought she had died and gone to heaven. Her parents sighed in relief, and they all rushed to put together something fast before she started to show and all the people in her parent's church found out, their worst nightmare, all caused by their wayward sinful daughter.

I still carry so much pain about that, she thought. They were far more concerned about what their friends and neighbors would think than anything I was feeling. I was the bad one whose disregard for how much they had given me all of my life now had the power to ruin their reputation. I had to push one part of me way down deep to be able to deal with it all. Sometimes I wonder if why I am so unhappy most of the time is because I never let that part of myself come up to really feel or express.

Of course she had to tell her OB-GYN about the herpes so they could make sure she didn't have an outbreak when delivery was imminent, as that can really hurt the child coming through the birth canal. Thank God her cool aunt was her family doctor, her father's sister who had gone her own way and had nothing to do with Catholicism any more. If it hadn't for her, she never would have gotten through it all.

Then Larry got transferred to the west coast pretty soon after the wedding and they moved right away, and so were able to get away with almost no one knowing in their old life she'd already been carrying, and made sure no one in their new life knew exactly when they'd gotten married. Their idea was to set it up so their child also would never know about it, something Larry was not so supportive of, but which I insisted on. In hindsight, I thought that was necessary because I still needed my parents in my life and needed to fake things up to preserve the picture and ensure there were no holes anywhere in the story.

After Mandy was born, the outbreaks came on regularly at least once a month and lasted over a week, and when it was twice a month you could kiss the whole month goodbye in terms of sex. It'd been a constant nerve-wracking hell to keep track of the early signs and make sure they didn't have sex if there was any risk at all. The longer time went on, the harder it was to get up the nerve to tell Larry about it. She was afraid he'd feel so lied to for so long that he'd leave for sure.

So I just made it seem like I wasn't so interested in sex whenever I wasn't sure if I might infect him, she thought, a small price to pay. It's worked for almost thirteen years now, and he never caught it, thank God. I'm sure he must think I just lost interest or fell out of love for him, which of course I didn't in either case. I just couldn't live with the chance of giving the only man who ever stood by me and loved me a dose of herpes, no way. But then I sort of got out of the habit of wanting sex altogether because there was always so much anxiety around it, and things just got cold in that area for me. And once that started to happen, it started to turn cooler in other parts of my life with him too. Inevitable, I guess.

I watched as he transferred some of his emotional needs to Mandy, our little ball of spunk and fire. It hurt so much to see how much they shared together after she started to talk, and I have had to work so hard to not resent her for that over the years. Then when she started to develop like a Playboy centerfold so early, I could see that because he was such a good man, Larry got tortured about how to deal with it all, with me not seeming interested in sex and Mandy beginning to give off such innocent and powerful sexual energy. Part of me was happy when he started to shut her out a few years ago, and I feel horrible about that. But Mandy's so smart I think she picked that up, and now that she's almost fourteen we're like strangers with each other.

Given her looks, it's a godsend that she has morals, although I don't know from where. Must have been inborn with her, because we sure haven't been heavy-handed with her about it, given our upbringings. Looking like she does and with all the attention she gets from older guys, it's amazing she still stays pretty much to herself and doesn't seem as interested in the parties thing and guys like her friend Carolyn. God, I love her so much.

And my parents .... most of the time it felt like they'd become my two other children! With my father showing signs of Alzheimer's and my mother's constant whining and calling me sometimes twice a day, it was torture to have to deal with them. But they had no one else to help them. They had had both her brother and her late in their life, and since Jack had told them where to stick it and left for who knows where almost nine years ago, now that they were getting old, there was only me for them to lean on.

Why does life have to be so hard?

What happened to how much her dreams used to light up the sense of her future? She was a good person, she knew that. But she could never close the gap between what she knew in her head was good about her and what was bad in how she actually felt about herself. Thoughts and emotions were very different things to her, even though most people said they were made of the same whatever and thoughts had the power to make bad emotions disappear, all the books said that. They never did that with her. What was wrong with her that they didn't, no matter how hard she had tried?

Maybe I need some therapy or an anti-depressant, she thought. My friend Jeff had done that Voice Dialogue thing. Maybe she should call him today and ask him about it. Anything was better than looking down the road of her whole life and seeing only grays and browns. Lately she had begun to feel like Dorothy in the Wizard of Oz stuck in her own black-and-white version of Kansas. As a child she had always imagined an Oz technicolor life where things were not perfect, but perfectly imperfect.

Where did those pictures go? she thought.

Into what dustbin of dreams do our deepest longings go when we get older and life seems to cover them over with a haze of lassitude? How did I turn from a hopeful, heartful, poetic little girl into a bored overweight woman who likes her Merlot a little too much? And why was it that even though I continue to feel everything on the inside so much, most of what comes out of my expressions with my family is cool and distant and like I always have a chip on my shoulder and resent them for living?

I will call Jeff today. I will. Maybe all I need is someone to talk to. If my mind can't seem to control my feelings, maybe a little picker-upper in a pill can help.

Just for awhile. Nothing permanent. She sighed, looked down at her coffee, and realized it had gotten cold.

Xiao-Ling

Xiao-Ling had always been a challenge for her father and mother. She was born both willful and sweetly wise, and that combination made it difficult for her parents to discipline her when needed. As a young girl, she was easily distracted by nature and often walked off from their home in the north of China, smitten merely by a scented breeze from the mountains or the noisy flight of a colorful bird. Many times they would search for her for hours until they found her sitting under a tree happily content looking up at the sky, and unaware of how long she had been gone or how worried her parents had been.

By the time she was fifteen, her father had had enough of her idiosyncratic oddity and lack of interest in the affairs of people, and sent her off to the south. Lau-Kueng, a well-to-do friend of the family, had agreed to take her in, give her employment, and find her a suitable husband. He gave her a room in the garden house behind The Floating Dragon, a high-end brothel he owned modeled after the legendary Japanese teahouses of the day. But it catered more to the flesh end of the spectrum rather than the artistic as establishments of that kind went. Lau-Kueng had given her a job of cleaning the rooms at The Floating Dragon in exchange for her food and board, for which she was absent-mindedly grateful in her own way.

Lau-Kueng was an avid Confucian living with his family in what is now Nanning during the relatively golden age of the cosmopolitan Tang Dynasty. He also traveled once a year to the Big Wild Goose pagoda near Xian to study Buddhism some four hundred years after Bodhidharma's arrival in China to introduce Ch'an Buddhism.

According to lore, the Big Wild Goose pagoda was named after a legend that told of how an early Buddhist sect at that location held that eating meat was not a taboo. One day, they couldn't find any meat to buy, and upon seeing a group of big wild geese flying by, a monk said to himself: 'Today we have no meat. I hope the merciful Bodhisattva will give us some.' At that very moment, the leading wild goose broke one of its wings and fell to the ground. All the monks were startled and believed that a Bodhisattva showed his spirit to order them to be more pious. They then established a pagoda on the site where the wild goose fell and promptly stopped eating meat.

Lau-Kueng thus fancied himself a philosopher and seeker in addition to his varied business interests. And he noticed right away there was something unusual about Xiao-Ling, so even though she was a lower-born girl from the north, he made time to talk with her and right away noted her peculiar air of uninvolved equanimity. He could not put her in any normal box of understanding that explained the range of her intelligence, casual aloofness, and her strange way with all kinds of animals, which seemed oddly attracted to her. And because she could read, unusual for a girl from that part of the country, he also invited her to use his modest esoteric library he had accumulated over time for his interests.

But Xiao-Ling had no interest in the written word, being too disengaged from mental focus to read much about anything, that seeming too small for her desire to be in life rather than wasting the time to study about life. Lau-Kueng thus set about finding her a husband, which, without a significant dowry, would be a challenge. As her guardian, he would of course put up something to maintain the family's face in that regard, but certainly did not intend to go overboard with this girl from the north enough to worry about enticing a more well-born mate and family.

She had also attracted the attention of a young man who worked at The Floating Dragon, a kitchen cleanup person, also lower-born. But his interest was strictly lustful, as Xiao-Ling was not unattractive. But Xiao-Ling found him dense and repellant and so did not return any of his overbearing invitations. This enraged the young man and delighted his two male friends who also worked on the grounds of The Floating Dragon, who took advantage of such a rare rejection of their friend's usual success with girls to poke fun at this failure.

One day Xiao-Ling was changing the linens on one of the beds, pushing the corner of a pillow into one corner of its pillowcase. As the pillow's corner fitted precisely into the corner of the pillowcase, she had a sudden rush of unfamiliar disorientation. Like a bubble breaking, she abruptly felt how all of separate life phenomena perceivable to the senses were simply 'wrappings' embedded within a surrounding Benign Benevolent Being that preceded and superceded the wrappings and as such, represented their deeper nature.

Just how the pillowcase created an artificial layer of experience between the pillow and the sleeper, what people experienced as normal sensate phenomena was entirely backlit by the deeper reality of the pillowness of this Benign Benevolent Being, which also connected all the seemingly separate phenomenal wrappings we called things into one universal wholeness. It was like this benign Benevolent Being had found a way to wrap Itself in thingness or separate pieces in order to know Itself to Itself in some way.

But it wasn't that the sense of separateness created by the wrapness was unreal in itself: the apparent separateness of things was just a one domain step-down from the Whole Oneness of the Benign Benevolent Being that contained all the separate 'pieces.' Xiao-Ling realized how all things, birds, sky, clouds, persons were thus all just wrappednesses embedded always within this Benign Benevolent Being. She wondered in her gradually slipping separateness if all things but people knew about this loving Presence.

Then Xiao-Ling collapsed on the floor of the room next to the bed, lost in a kind of universalized rapture as she felt herself retain her own personally wrapped nature while also floating within the loving supportive sea of the Benign Benevolent Being. Another one of the maids found her lying there a few minutes later and called the headwoman, who had Xiao-Ling carried back to her room.

The young man who had been spurned by her saw them through a window of the Inn's kitchen as they took her away, asked the headwoman what had happened, and was told she had just collapsed and was helpless even though she was awake and seemed fine. When she remained in this state for the better part of that day and the next, a doctor was called but could not find anything wrong: her pulses were strong and her wrists had no telltale malodor.

Being her guardian, Lau-Kueng was also alerted, but by the time he arrived Xiao-Ling was sitting upright and smiling. The change in her was remarkable, as if her casual aloofness and equanimity had now been deepened and extended. After hearing her retell what had happened with her, Lau-Kueng had her gather her belongings and set out with her at once for Xian and the Big Wild Goose pagoda.

Ten days later she was sitting in front of Master Honghui, the leader of the temple, with Lau-Kueng in attendance. After asking her to repeat what she had said to Lau-Kueng. Honghui studied her in silence for many minutes, and then said, "The Great Buddha tells us that the Being you speak of is not experiencable, a No-Thing out of which all other apparency arises, including the Benevolence you describe. How is it you say you can experience it?"

"I cannot speak of what the Buddha says, whoever he is," Xiao-Ling replied.

"It is my opinion, however remarkable what happened to you, since it is still an experience registered as such by the person, it does not qualify for enlightenment according to true Ch'an Buddhism," Honghui replied, looking directly at Lau-Kueng.

"I do not care what you say it is or what it isn't," said Xiao-Ling, without malice but without the formal politeness and respect expected of her when speaking to Master Honghui.

"Everything is Nothing, and Nothing is Everything," said Honghui, growing impatient with what he saw as arrogance in an ignorant peasant girl.

"Everything is Something, but Source is Mystery-Love," replied Xiao-Ling.

"Perhaps she should remain with you, Master Honghui," said Lau-Kueng hastily, trying to save face for her and himself. "Maybe she has gone part of the way on her own with no training, and could go further if aided."

"Out of the question," replied Honghui, made angry by her impertinence. "No person could go that far with no training, much less an ignorant girl. And Siddartha taught that women cannot enlighten because of their weak nature, and this one is obviously no exception."

"Excuse me, Master, but does not your own temple story speak of a Bodhisattva answering the prayers of the monks, implying consciousness endures in the hereafter as a middle place on its way to the nothing of Nirvana?"

Master Honghui snorted. "Such nonsense is only the holdover of mystical Hinduism overlaying the teachings of the Lion of the Shakyas, held onto by less clear lineages. Here at Big Wild Goose pagoda, we follow the teachings of Hui-neng, the Sixth Patriarch of Ch'an, who, when another monk wrote:

> 'The body is a bodhi-tree.
> The mind is a standing mirror bright:
> At all times polish it diligently
> And allow no dust to alight.'

Hui-neng wrote in reply ....:

> 'No wisdom tree exists,
> Nor the stand of mirror bright.
> Since all is empty from the beginning.
> Where can any dust alight?'

.... and became the new head monk by virtue of his deeper truth. Any belief in something as anything is thus unenlightened," Honghui stated confidently.

"Ah, yes .... thank you, Master Honghui. Perhaps she could stay on as a Buddhist nun to help with the sangha?" replied Lau-Kueng.

"I think not," said Honghui, eyeing her suspiciously. "The feng-shui around her head is disturbing to me, she is impertinent, and she would be a distraction to the monks because of her odd beauty. Take her back with you, although it now may be even more difficult to find her a husband." With that, Master Honghui rose to end the audience, noting as he left the room that Xiao-Ling had been wholly disinterested in their conversation, preferring to watch a hummingbird flit close to the window and gaze out onto the pagoda grounds, while the two men talked about her as if she were not in the room.

Lau-Kueng sighed heavily and reluctantly began the long journey back to Nanning with her.

Upon her return, Xiao-Ling was told to take a week to rest, which she happily agreed to, spending the days exploring the forest behind The Floating Dragon and returning before dusk. But on the fourth day, she was interrupted as she sat under a tree by the young man from the kitchen and his two friends, who had followed her into the forest on their day off. Xiao-Ling was surprised, but sensing the Benign Benevolent Being within which the three young men were embedded, she simply acknowledged them with a smile and went back to contemplating the caterpillar she had been playing with in her palm.

The boy who had been spurned by her stepped closer, slapped the insect out of her hand, and roughly pulled her up. "You have time for me now, yes?" He then insolently ripped off her clothing as she struggled to resist, at first unable to take in what was happening. The three young men then had their way with her, in the three means possible men can be with women, each of them simultaneously violating her in those three ways.

She thrashed and fought as she felt the indescribable pain and horror of so many women over the centuries at the hands of physically stronger men of neanderthalic consciousness driven by patriarchal power, disdainful disregard, or sexual satiation, utterly unmindful and uncaring about the suffering they so casually delivered to the woman. Of course karma would always have the final word in what lay in future lives for such bestial unheartful men. But that had always been scarce solace to the uncountable number of women in the narrative of humanity made to endure such evil and torture at the hands of drooling, arrogant, and brutalizing men.

Xiao-Ling could not even cry out in her pain, because the young man who had been originally interested in her had his member in her mouth and would not remove it while he tightly closed her nose with one hand and held her jaw locked just open enough that she could not bite down with the other, choking her. She could not breathe, and could not get free of the hold the three young men had her in. After a short time she stopped struggling and went slack.

As she suffocated and died, she felt the Presence of the Benevolent Being envelop her warmly and directly. Her body dropped away, a golden light buoyed her away from the scene, and the one formerly known as Xiao-Ling merged with the Infinite while remaining enough of a mote of her finite nature of consciousness within Infinity to realize what was happening.

Maker

Lucipha-el had completed his TERP and was standing in the staging area that preceded entrance to the Throne Room. He tingled in anticipation for the audience with Maker he was called to while in the middle of his annual debate with his first advisor Ankha-el about the essence of Divine Being. When the Celestial Horns played by the Micha-el-ites burst forth their purple reverberation, the doors slowly opened, and Lucipha-el walked into Maker's abiding Space.

As always, he was aware of the Presence-Backlight of Maker's Mate the Nondual, with which all of Maker's expressiveness was intimately and equally linked. The Great Nondual Yinther never spoke, It Be-ing That Which allowed space for Maker's expressivity to move.

This silence spawned endless jokes in the Lucipha-el kingdom about how the noisy Yangther and Its silent Nondual Mate ever got together to make all the ang-els. These jokes were considered profane by the Micha-el-ites, embraced tentatively by the Gabra-el-ites, but enjoyed heartily by the Lucipha-el-ites, they of the most base density but also the most complex ang-el nature.

"Good millennia, Lucipha-el my son," thundered Maker. Maker did not actually speak loudly, but when in such proximity to It, even It's slightest expression was far 'louder' than an ang-el was used to when ensconced in their home vibratory ang-el realm reality. Lucipha-el winced, and said, "Greetings, Yangther! May all of Creation rejoice in the glory of Your .... ."

"You can skip the usual litany of honorifics today, son," replied Maker. "We have big medicine to discuss."

Lucipha-el was a little shocked, but when The Boss says 'Jump!' you say 'How high?' What Lucipha-el didn't and couldn't know at that moment was that It would soon be saying 'Fall!' and Lucipha-el saying, 'How low?'

"The time has come for the answer to the debate between you and Ankha-el's about Love and Will," Maker boomed.

Lucipha-el was even more shocked, because never had Maker directly given an answer to any question put out by the ang-els. Always It required them to elicit the answer for themselves within the aegis of their own experience. "Yangther, this is such a surprise!" he said. "Please, I await your Wisdom!"

Maker knitted the brow It didn't have, and said, "What I mean is, enough time for the philosophical debate has passed. It is time now for the question to be explored in another way, a more lived-into crucible of dialogue, disputation, and distribution."

"Oh," replied Lucipha-el, a bit disappointed, but also intensely interested. "I am in your service," he replied.

Maker sighed. "I know, son. It is for that reason I need to ask something of you that will be very difficult."

Difficult? Lucipha-el thought. What could be difficult about personally serving a directive from Maker Itself? However hard it might be, by doing so he would then be within an extremely intense energetic stream of direct connect with his Yangther that would link him deeply to It at all times while he was performing the duty. In effect, personal service to Maker was like an extended PPP that enlivened him in ways no other dynamism could. Doing a direct errand for It was always thus accompanied by that kind of buoyant energetic influx and uplift, and even after the duty was discharged, aspects of that energetic remained with the ang-el as a permanent part of the being.

"Tell me, Yangther, and Your Will be done."

Maker began, "When your Yinther and I created our first Child of Be-ing, the Micha-el-ites, and their first-born and leader Micha-el, self-sentient consciousness was born. It was wonderful to stir the pot of our Love-Light and bake it through to a way for separate be-ing and consciousness to co-participate simultaneously in group be-ing and consciousness. We were of course very pleased with them and their lightness and love."

Lucipha-el nodded. The more yinified Micha-el-ites were like what later would be called bees in a hive or ants in a colony, a kind of group soul made up of independent be-ings with energetic bodies of their own as expressions of their consciousness, whose edges of one never lost contact with the edges of all the others.

"Then your Yinther and I added a bit more individuation dynamic to the mix and cooked through the heavier, more yangified Gabra-el-ites and their first-born Gabra-el, whose independent be-ing of self-sentience was even more condensed, with Wisdom-Will as their inbred theme," Maker continued.

Where was this headed, Lucipha-el thought? This story was of course well-known to all the ang-els. Unlike Micha-el-ites, Gabra-el-ites were more separately independent but still linked, more like what later would be called eagles, who often flocked together but also were more alone in themselves. There must be some specific reason for It to be relating all of it to me right now.

"Then, being pleased so well with our second Child of be-ing, we then set out to add even more condensed individuational dynamisms, flavoring our third and heaviest Child of Be-ing with equal yin-yang valences and the inbred theme of Patience-Balance. WE named you all the Lucipha-el-ites, with you as their first born and leader, and again we were much pleased."

"I am glad you made me, Yangther," Lucipha-el replied. "And may I say, it was brilliant to distill the Yin-Love-Light of the Micha-el-ites and Yang-Wisdom-Will of the Gabra-el-ites and endow us with aspects of both. Unlike the ease with which they who have but one valence to embody, it is often difficult for us Lucipha-el-ites to find an inner peace between these two elemental aspects of be-ing that seem to not easily co-exist. But when we occasionally succeed in doing so, our consciousness vibrates in ways that are bi-chromatic and always creatively and powerfully disseminative. Good art!"

"Yes .... your Yinther and I did that for a reason, son," Maker replied, with just a hint of sadness.

Lucipha-el of course picked that up and asked, "Why are You so sad, Yangther?"

"Because you will very much need that disseminative and balanced bi-chromatic creativity to be successful on your long journey to the answer you and Ankha-el have so passionately sought," It replied, with even more sorrow transporting Its words.

"Yes, Yangther. Tell me where I shall go."

"You will go where no self-sentient consciousness has ever been."

This stunned Lucipha-el. The whole of Creation was comprised of the three ang-el realms, and they were already populated by self-sentient ang-els. There was no level of be-ing that did not possess self-sentient consciousness.

"Excuse me Yangther, I do not understand."

Maker sighed again, even more deeply. "I know, son. Bide with me...your Yinther and Yangther made you and your ang-el clan for a very specific destiny, very unlike the Micha-el-ites and Gabra-el-ites. That destiny involves the final outworking of your issue of Love versus Will, and to attain that, to create homes for countless other Child-Beings of our creation that we plan to make soon."

Lucipha-el was completely confused, which was a previously unknown state of consciousness for him. He then again felt that shiver, the forebodance he'd had about Ankh-el's one-third conscription of the other ang-els to his Maker-as-Will-based cause.

"We know how hard it is for you, the heaviest and most dense ang-el, and thus the Lucipha-el-ite with the most defined edge-truth, to hold your brother and sister Lucipha-el-ites within the angel realm that includes the Micha-el-ites and Gabra-el-ites. We want you to rest from that burden and incept another mission of be-ing."

"But how shall I do that?" Lucipha-el answered, puzzled. "In order to not hold the bottom of our realm to balance the effect of the magnepole of the Mich-al-ites to you, and thus maintain the Gabra-el-ites in equilibrium, I would have to .... ."

"Let go?" Maker answered, completing his sentence.

"I was going to say....I don't know what I was going to say. Let go? But .... there is nothing beneath my domain to 'let go' into. I am confused. Please forgive my ignorance."

"It is not ignorance, Luc. A new configuration is at hand, and you were created to be the one to begin it, see it through its evolution in the answering of the question of Love versus Will, and complete it as you return to me." Maker took a breath, and said, "You, as the most condensed and edged Lucipha-el-ite, will let go and fall from the angel domains to pave an energetic path for all of the Lucipha-el-ites to seed multiple new levels of Consciousness Be-ing, the lightest one-tenth of your clan falling the least away from Us, the heaviest one-tenth the farthest from Us, and the middle four-fifths spread out between, according to their relative densities."

Maker paused so Lucipha-el-ite could absorb what It had said.

Trying hard to not be overwhelmed by the picture Maker was painting, Lucipha-el tried to envision it. Even though Micha-el-ites were the least dense ang-els, Gabr-el-ites the next, and Lucipha-el-ites the most, all three ang-el domains, each within themselves also had a sub-range of ang-el densities. Like the other two ang-el realms, Lucipha-el-ite ang-els had a range of their own from least dense to most dense, with Lucipha-el and a segment of his kin representing the most dense.

What Maker seemed to be saying was that him letting go of his capacity to hold the most dense ang-el realm within the overall ang-el domain would result in the Lucipha-el-ites carving out new domains of consciousness, the distance from the other two ang-el realms a function of the range of Lucipha-el-ite densities. Wait, he thought, and then began to feel a stark terror: Maker said I and the densest Lucipha-el-ites would fall the farthest? Does that mean I will never again be able to ....?

Maker began again before Lucipha-el could complete his thought. "After these multiple new levels are seeded and held by the density range of Lucipha-elic ang-el array, your Yinther and I will create uncountable numbers of Child Be-ings vibratorily resonant with each of the levels held by what will then be the ancestor seed-soul Lucipha-el-ites in each, living in each level."

Trying to understand the picture and manage his emotion at the same time was too much for Lucipha-el. He put up his hand to Maker, something he had not ever done before, and said, "Yangther, please.... .stop for a moment. I .... I, need some time to .... ."

"Yes, son." Maker replied, and was prepared to wait for eternity until Lucipha-el had fully grokked the situation.

Lucipha-el roiled within from the swirl of emotion and vision imparted by Maker's words. The panorama of the picture was incredible to see: the entire Lucipha-el realm would drop out of the angel domain and seed multiple levels of new Consciousness Be-ing, each level established according to the varying density level of the Lucipha-el-ites, the least dense dropping the least distance and establishing one new level there, the next next, and so on, until all the Lucipha-el-ites had dropped to a level consonant with their density, Lucipha-el and his densest brethren having fallen the farthest.

Then Maker and Its Mate would secondarily create new souls whose vibratory valences would match each of the levels held by each density level of the Lucipha-el-ites, who would hold that level of vibration as seed-souls until all the new Child Be-ings of that density arrived, and then assumedly care for them until they were acclimated to their new existence. What an astounding idea .... his Yangther and Yinther had decided to create new souls of even more edgeness-density than the Lucipha-el-ites, and the Lucipha-el-ites had been originally created to be the seed-soul holders of the new domains in which they would live, in an ever-increasing density array.

"Yes," Maker replied, to his thoughts.

Lucipha-el barely heard his Yangther as his heart-mind was still spinning. Each subsequently dense level would refract the Love-Light of Maker and Its Mate in its own different orchestration of color and sound, creating a dazzling rainbow of Be-ing, all moving from the deeper-lighter waters of Divine Being to Its shallower-denser waters, but still all held within Divine Being equally.

"Yes again," said Maker. "Everything will abide equally within our Divine Being. But in the densest level, it will be very difficult to experience that."

And then it hit him: he himself and his densest brethren, ensconced in the shallowest, densest waters of the new array, would experience themselves as farthest away from the Presence of Divine Being. Did that mean that their density level would be so far away that the Presence's presence would be reduced in their direct experience to that degree? Meaning Lucipha-el and his densest brethren, despite knowing Maker could never not be, would actually feel a loss of deep connection to It in their awareness?

"Yes, son," It sorrowfully replied. "You will."

The heart aspect of Lucipha-el's heart-mind seemed to explode then as a nova of pain and despair detonated in his center. This was the forebodance he felt, for which he had no understanding until now. How can I live without Presence's presence? I know I could never be outside of Its Be-ing, as nothing can be outside its Creator's Providence, but I will then be so much less warmed and lighted by how much further from It I will be!

"It will seem very cold and dark, yes," Maker said, again to his unspoken words. "You will suffer greatly from this."

The third archangel seemed to collapse under the burden of what was being asked of him. How can I bear the loss of my archangelic brothers and all the other angels? What do I call upon in myself to hold my heart-mind in clear enough ways to fulfill my duty? How will I keep warm in such a cold, distant, and shallow place? On whom will I depend?

"We will wait for as long as it takes for you to consider this, my son," Maker assured him. "No matter how long. But it must occur."

Lucipha-el felt the truth of his Yangther's words: Maker would wait an eternity if need be. Feeling that patient space transported to him how much his Yangther loved him, and how much It must believe him able to do this duty, even though he himself did not share that confidence.

After being with that for a time, Lucipha-el slowly raised his head and spoke, "Yangther, I fear I am neither Loving nor Willful enough and so ill-equipped to do this service .... perhaps it is best if Micha-el or Gabra-el do this for you."

"No," Maker replied. "They must always remain in their respective realms to hold the angel domain together. They are not part of this new configuration, and neither of them possess the necessary density to carve out the space for the new levels of Consciousness Be-ing such that your Yinther and I can then plant the new soul children within it." It paused. "There is more to the service I haven't yet described."

More, thought Lucipha-el? I can barely hold what It has said to me so far. But he rallied and said, "Tell me all that you ask of me."

"The farther from Us you fall, the more dense and edged the level of Consciousness becomes, as you have seen. At the bottom, where you will call yourselves humang-els, the edges and densenesses will be such that the Love-Light and Wisdom-Will of our Divine Being barely reaches to these depths. Only in that darkness and cold, which is still within Divine Being but seeming not, will creation find whether it be Love or Will that is the Essence of our Divine Being."

"But why will that be so?" asked Lucipha-el.

"Because only in that darkest, coldest, and shallowest place will the struggle be deeply sufficient enough to live the answer into being, and not just debate it as is the only possibility in less dense domains."

"Ah .... ," said Lucipha-el. "I feel I begin to understand."

Maker smiled broadly with the face It did not possess. "What you just said, 'I feel I begin to understand' is the rock of the base and the wings of the expression you will impart to your service, to the question, and to the end result."

"I do not know what you mean, but I will drink of what you say."

"Know that as each new level of Consciousness Be-ing is established, the singular question of Will versus Love will be the governing dynamic that will drive all the impulses of the new souls in each level to survive, to grow, and to prosper. The amelioration of that conflict will create tidal waves of difficulty, and what is only friendly debate in the ang-el realms about it will escalate to deeper and deeper forms of conflict the edgier and more dense the new levels evolve."

"At times the conflict will threaten the very fabric of their souls and the worlds they create. But when you, as my son, live among them for the many millennia that this service will require, and learn with them through your own lived truth and the lived truths of others, you will be the one to first and finally embody the answer, and when you do, you, having fallen the farthest, will then turn around and lead all our children back to Us through the power and love of your be-ing."

"And .... the friendly debate between you and Ankha-el, who accompanies you to the most dense level, will intensify to the same degree of which I have spoken. Those children souls who believe Love is more essential will see Ankha-el as the evil one who fights against Divine Being, calling him Shaitan. And you, who hold the opposite, will be invisible to almost all of those who believe Will is more essential, as the worlds they create will be based in that and will thus see you and your message as weak and without merit. There will also be those most confused by the chaos of the outworking of this question who will mistakenly call you, Lucipha-el the Light-Giver, Shaitan in error, not knowing it is you to whom I have given this sacred service, and in the end, to be the deliverer of the answer."

"But .... I already hold one side of the question, that Love is Your Essence. If I am to be the one to deliver the answer, is it not already complete?" asked Lucipha-el.

"No," Maker replied. "For in those darker, colder, and shallower places, feeling alone and without my countenance, you yourself will be confused as to the true answer, and shall need many cycles of be-ing to finally know. You will need Will for many eons so that the new humang-els can survive, and Love will seem distant in those times. In that way, Ankha-el will harbor no such doubts about his position, and many characteristics of the most dense domains will support his conclusions. That he will not have doubt, but that you will, shall cause a great chasm to form between you two, until you finally embody the answer and lead all in all levels back to Me and your Yinther."

Maker paused, then said, "Only one who finally embodies the an-swer to Will or Love being primary after being tested in the most egre-giously difficult dense domain of Be-ing, is thus qualified to bring all the others in question forward to me. And when that is done, all of Creation will embody the Truth of Be-ing inherent in existence, where Consciousness abides in the One as it travels ever in the Many."

With this, Lucipha-el finally gestalted the service overall, but could not yet absorb all of its ramifications. "I accept, Yangther. May I have a short time to prepare? The heart aspect of my heart-mind groks, but the mind aspect does not."

"You may. Your Yinther and I have many arrangements to make before the Rise, so the time is merited."

"The 'Rise?'" Is it not a Fall, Yangther?"

"It will seem like a Fall, but it is actually a Rise to Wholeness, as the Many who remain eternally Self-ed will then be able to have their edged Selfs and the One together. In that way, the level you will in-habit will be the 'lowest' structural level of be-ing, but the 'highest' experiential level of be-ing."

"I do not grok ....?" said Lucipah-el.

"Only from your densest level of be-ing, which shall be called Erath Logos, will all other dimensions of experience in all the new lev-els of Consciousness created by your Lucipha-elic Rise be experienca-ble. Only inhabitants of a level of consciousness that is lower will be able to learn to experience the levels which are higher: the levels which are higher than others cannot experience the consciousness of those that are lower unless they cycle down inhabitively to them. Ang-els cannot experience Erath Logoan's experience without cycling there to live, but Erath Logoans will be able to learn how to experience ang-el consciousness from their domain after you teach them."

"Thus, many Micha-el-ites and Gabra-el-ites, but not Micha-el or Gabra-el, will eventually join you there to learn to experience your Yinther and I from that most difficult and dense domain. And because the Erath Logos level will be so far away from We the Source, your Yinther and I decided to curve the entire array such that the densest level will actually be backed right up rear-ward to the least dense Micha-el-ites, who will much love the Erath Logoans and act as their invisible guardians from behind to help them in that most difficult of domains to remember their legacy of soul and origin."

"Yes, Yangther. I do not yet understand fully, but I will."

"A few more guidances, my son. When you and your Lucipha-el-ite brethren were created, you fell the 'farthest' from Us, relative to the other two realms, yes?"

Lucipha-el nodded. "I remember, that when I first awoke as being self-ed and 'fell' away from You and my Yinther, I recognized I was coming 'out' of one part of You but going into another part of You. I was afraid, in what felt like three contractions. But when I arrived in our realm and felt You and Yinther still near, the fear was lost."

"Yes," replied Maker. Those three contractions of fear were not fully expressive because you landed proximal enough to us to allay them. But remnants of them remain in you. When the new configuration begins to develop and the levels of Consciousness Be-ing increase in edgeness, density, and darkness, the souls your Yinther and I make will not have the solace of our proximal Presence. This means those three contractions of fear, common to all self-sentience, will increase and deepen the farther the distance from Source those souls are birthed."

"These three contractions must be healed in order for all the new souls to be able to ever return to the Source and thus be fully balanced in both Self and One. This means the issue of Will versus Love will pivot upon and be inextricably linked to these fears and their healing. You will have to create the means for this healing to occur. You will need to live many cycles of Self-ed be-ing to create that means, but create it you must."

"Yes, Yangther. Can you tell me the three fears?"

"No: encountering what they are will be part of your lived experience and your ideas for their healing. After many cycles you will create the means to identify and heal these three contractions, which are related to the Yinther, to Me, and to Self-ed-ness, the child of both of Us. You will find the means and embody access to your Yinther first, using Will to lose Will, and become known for all time for this."

"Then shortly after, in another cycle, you will create and embody the means to access Me, using Love to gain Love, and also be known for all time. And finally, after many more cycles have passed, you will create and embody the means to access the truth of Self-ed-ness, using light-forms of Love to change dark forms of Will, and light-forms of Will to change dark forms of Love. In all three shall you be in the form of the Yang-being vehicular expression in solitude to do this, but in the second and third will be joined by a Yin-being vehicular expression as co-teacher and companion."

Maker sighed. "By means of these three embodiments shall you then heal the three contractions of soul-birth, answer the question of Will versus Love as primary, link the Yangther, the Yinther, and their Child of Divine Be-ing entire, and thus bring all of our new children home to Us by showing them how to do what you have discovered."

"Yes, Yangther."

"Also: unlike the ang-el realms, the energy bodies of the denser levels of be-ing that will be the expression of the new Self-ed souls will require more weight and edge-ness and so will not be directly created by Us, but by the Children souls themselves. In that way, your Yinther and I will create the consciousness of each child-soul, but the vehicular expression of the consciousness will be provided by a mechanism of the vehicular expression itself."

"I do not grok, my Yangther."

"It is like the Copulangelional Conjugative Connubiality you ang-els enjoy ..... "

"And for which we are eternally grateful!"

"Yes .... but instead of only the joyful intensity of sharing being the result, the CCC of the denser levels can also result in the creation of a new vehicular expression of a new child-soul, created out of the Love and Will of an older Yin and Yang pair."

The idea astounded Lucipha-el. When ang-els participated in CCC, no new ang-els were produced, as all the ang-els had already been created by Yangther and Yinther. Yangther was saying here that new expressions of the energy bodies of the new soul-children can also be produced in such an activity. He exclaimed, "What art! Then the two older Yin and Yang recapitulate You and Yinther in that domain for that purpose, to make expressions for new souls!" He thought a moment, trying to envision it. "I think I might like that," he said.

Maker shook the head It did not possess, and said, "You have no idea .... in addition, since the vehicular energy bodies will be part of the dense level of be-ing they will be shed after a time, and you will acquire a fresh one later to continue your journey. And one last thing: the issue of Love and Will as the Essence of Divine Being will become the critical dynamic in the transaction of their form of CCC, which they will call Soulful Erotic Kinetic Salacity, or SEKS. Souls will be very confused if it be Will or Love that primarily drives the exchanges, as will you. If you can remember this, living into the dynamisms of SEKS will yield clues as to the answer you will be seeking."

"I will try to remember, my Yangther."

"And last, and this is extremely important .... unlike the ang-el domains where you all live a dynamism of 'undercome,' in the denser and edgier domains they who believe Will is the Essence of Be-ing will create an 'overcome' dynamism of be-ing, and those who believe Love is the Essence of Be-ing will create a dynamism of 'undergo.' Will versus Love in the more edged and dense domains shall thus become an expressed issue of 'overcoming' versus 'undergoing' dynamisms in response to the challenges of dense life. It will be well for you to remember this in your worlds that lie ahead."

"Yes, Yangther. I shall remember this. But it is difficult for me to imagine splitting our natural ang-elic 'undercome' way of living into the versions of 'overcome' and 'undergo.' And what about the other possibility, that of 'overgo?'"

"You do not miss much, son. They who most deeply abide with 'overcome' dynamisms will create an even deeper version of 'overgo.'" They who do this will create the most chaos before the resolution you create. But remember, countless configurations of be-ing must be constructed to work through the question, and chaos will be the necessary force to dissemble any specific form on the way to create a new one. Embrace both chaos and creation as equal poles in your worlds, but know that in the end it is always darkest before the dawn."

"I will remember, Yangther."

Then Lucipha-el noticed a twinkle in the eye It did not possess.

"What is it, Yangther?"

Maker smiled with the mouth It did not have, and said, "Sometimes it will seem like there is someone else in the mirror beside you."

"'Mirror'? What is a 'mirror'?" Lucipha-el replied.

"Just something you humang-els will make that will help you solve the Love-Will puzzle." With that, Maker rose with the legs It did not possess, indicating the audience was ended.

Lucipha-el rose also, but asked, "Yangther, please, one more question. How shall I make the Rise/Fall occur?"

Maker smiled again. "Just relax and let go, and trust, that in the end, letting go will always be the means of completing your service. But once you embody your new worlds, you must remember to let go only after you have toiled mightily and exhausted all means to create your worlds in the ways you feel right. If you let go too soon, it will be a dead-end. Many will feel the way is to let go before you wholify, but this will be error. Others will feel the way is to always toil without letting go, but that too will be an equal error. And even though we will regularly be in contact all though your journeys and a bit more directly in between your vehicular energy body sheddings, we cannot be with each other in this direct way until all the cycles complete."

There was a long pause as Lucipha-el took that in as fully as he could. The unknown of the experience that lay ahead of him was balanced by a curiosity in the change it would make in him. Worlds within worlds within worlds .... how will we find his way? Will he remember enough, and be soulfully wise and loving enough?

But in a flash he realized he was envisioning experience that was Not Yet, something he had never done before, because nothing was Not in his existence in the ange-el realms. He was thus the first angel and sentient consciousness to do this. How strange, and how interesting, he thought.

"Yes Lucipha-el," replied Maker to his silent musing. You will need such a Not Yet envisioning in your journeys. So until we meet again, Godspeed on your journey."

Lucipha-el smiled within and raised his eyes to his Parent.

"Yes, Yangther .... until we meet again."

Stephanie

"Will there ever be an end to all these tears?" Stephanie asked the therapist.

The white walls of the office merged with the clouds outside, making her feel as if she was floating in a prison of soft cotton, absorbing whatever emotional colors flowed out of her. She'd sentenced herself to voluntary incarceration here, once a week for seven months now, for the crime of choosing to change, a prison you go to help set you free, she thought. But all the tears had not made the new direction her life had taken these past eighteen months any more bearable. She'd endured alienation from most of her social and spiritual support group, agonal separation from her husband and children, and unrelenting attack from her own family. And, hardest of all, there was a terrifying gulf growing in her heart now separating her from God.

For eleven years she'd been the faithful wife of a Christian minister. Through the endless bustle of church work, she'd held her family together, protecting them and herself from the satanic influences of these end-times. She was taught that if you couldn't find a scriptural answer to any question of life, you were asking the wrong question.

Above all, you never listened to your own mind. That's where Satan seduced you most, steering you toward selfishness and away from serving the needs of others. Hadn't she seen the effects of that kind of straying, with the breakup of families, the cultural pull of all-consuming materialism, new age mysticism, and the satanic sexual messages bombarding us from every direction? That it was so difficult to conform to the Christian ideal was due to original sin, and only fervent prayer and surrender to the saving grace of the blood of Jesus atoned for our sinful humanity.

She couldn't pinpoint exactly when her faith had begun to unravel, like a spool of yarn that could never be rewound again. Was it the hypocrisy of Christians who preached one way and acted another, the spiritual elitism of those boasting they were saved, or the materialism of televangelists promising wealth as a reward for sending money to charismatic preachers with ivory-capped teeth?

She remembered vividly one Sunday when it had suddenly occurred to her that Christians were becoming the new Pharisees, with their insistence on the letter of the law and their harsh treatment of those who dared to question scripture. Hadn't Jesus endured just that kind of animosity at the hands of the Pharisees who thought only their Torah contained the truth? Feeling afraid that the supposed followers of Christ had become exactly what Jesus had criticized had shaken her faith to the marrow.

She had sought counseling initially because of her husband's continuing infidelity. The women were always younger, always those who needed counseling from someone wiser in the ways of the Lord. She could never understand how he could so fervently denounce the sins of the flesh from the pulpit yet find them so appealing with someone other than his wife. It was why they had to move so frequently, why he was always looking for a new church to pastor. He had always begged for her forgiveness after each transgression, vowing to change, always trying to wrestle from himself this satanic influence.

But she'd come to realize he actually enjoyed the fact Satan had chosen him to tempt, as that seemed to prove to him he was doing the Lord's work so well he'd come to the personal attention of the enemy. It never occurred to her she could do anything but stoically stand by him and pray for the strength to endure her burden.

But over time she could no longer accept a situation that would never change, no matter how hard she prayed for resolution. As she began to protest, he responded she didn't know how to forgive like Jesus. He had refused any secular counseling, maintaining the only counsel he needed was with his savior. But if that was the solution, why hadn't it worked after all these years?

Stephanie had found warmth and solace with this therapist, in spite of her humanist orientation. She didn't seem at all to be dominated by Satan, despite her husband's opinion that was exactly what satan wished her to think. She had given her courage to think about things in ways she'd never dared to think before. Whole new ways of looking at the landscape of her life were opening up to her. She was learning how much of her world had been designed for her by her father, who'd also been a pastor, and how thoroughly she'd been willing to live in that world. He had heartily approved of her decision to wed another man of God, and was also of the opinion she was mad and in danger of losing her soul for leaving her husband and family.

Through therapy, she was beginning to realize it had always been males to whom she had given the power to decide her fate: her father, her husband, or Jesus. That was how the bible described the roles between men and women. Now everything she'd ever held dear had been thrown into confusion, with no remaining solid base of understanding as a bulwark against doubt, no automatic Christian recipe for addressing life's challenges.

Was this bewildering state proof she was outside of God's providence, that she was a child of Satan now, as her family insisted? In spite of her new insights, the voices of her past religious indoctrination continued to torture her. It was almost as if the more her new awareness brought light into her world, the more darkness she never knew existed there was painfully exposed to sight.

"They'll end when the reservoir of emotion from which they flow is emptied," replied the therapist.

"But I've cried myself to sleep every night for years, and now I come here and cry more. I thought therapy was supposed to make me feel better."

"As we've said, good therapy is not about making you feel better, it's about making you feel more real, about feeling more worthy of your own truth. For years you've been crying in frustration over a situation you couldn't change, and now you cry from the confusion and hurt that comes from changing it. Can you see the progress in that?"

"Oh, sure," Stephanie replied. "Suffering is what I've always been great at. Show the world a brave and happy face in spite of your pain. Suffering is your badge of courage! Live in agony now to earn eternity with Jesus later. Oh, God …. why didn't I ever feel like I was supposed to feel?" she cried.

The therapist let her anguish. She knew each tear emptied more of the repository of dammed pain stored up over a lifetime. As it was with all the people in cults she tried to help in her deprogramming practice, her religion had been a drug used against the challenge of living on earth, her inner emptiness unconsciously drawn to the institutionalized self-unworthiness taught so deliberately by Christianity. How could anyone in this day and age not realize a belief in original sin forever denied them self-worth, the penalty of hell reserved for those daring to live by the sacredness of their own truth? How religion then actually functioned as a new obstacle to emotional health? She knew clearly how addiction to cultic spiritual belief systems paralleled that of alcohol and drugs, and how the same emotional wounds created both.

The therapist recalled how her own grandparents had often taken her to their own Christian services, wanting to make sure she didn't lose her soul as had her atheistic parents. She remembered one Sunday in particular when a young boy about her age was baptized. The look on that boy's face had always remained with her.

Even at that age, she'd realized the piety in his face came only from, could only come from, the approval he received from his family that day, and not from any true spiritual feeling of which a child was not yet capable. Later, she remembered that face on her own wedding day. Wish I'd noticed the significance of that then, she thought.

Her client's returning composure allowed her to continue.

"Remember last time how we were talking about choice?"

"You mean how everything we create for ourselves in life comes from the choices our unconscious subselves make?"

"Yes. But who made the conscious choices?"

"One of my subselves, right? Who else?"

The therapist didn't reply, and Stephanie knew that meant she needed to look deeper.

"What do you want to hear? If my life situation is the result of my choices, and my subselves make up who I know as me, me, then one of my subselves made the choices that resulted in my situation."

"I don't want to 'hear' anything, but the subselves made the unconscious choice, remember? Who made the conscious ones?"

Stephanie closed her eyes, trying to feel out the answer rather than get it from her head as she had been shown. She had learned these past months she wasn't as stupid as both her father and husband had insisted for so many years. The answers in her life had always been provided by someone or something else other than her. But if she gave the power to others to do the choosing for her life, then by default she herself wasn't. And if she wasn't choosing her own life, what did that make her? Some sort of non-player in life, some kind of non-person. Because if you're not the active agent of choice in life, didn't that make you something not real?

Without thinking, she blurted out, "No one made any conscious choices."

"Exactly," said the therapist, sighing.

Stephanie's eyes widened. She didn't have a real self! She had never had one! She had become the perfect product of the teaching that self was evil. Being saved was about never building a self. It instead relied on Jesus or Scripture or the Church to supply that role and function. Her entire expression of self centered around giving herself away to others, as she had been taught. Without those others to give unconditional love to and take care of, she didn't exist. She had given herself totally to God, as atonement for her original sin. Wasn't this the only way to heaven? Not having a selfish self? Hadn't she always tried to live this spiritual truth?

"So if you haven't determined the way of your choosing, what does that make you?"

"Some kind of nobody, someone not really real. All my life I've been taught to give myself away! To God, to my father, to my husband, to Jesus, to everyone but me! Isn't that what religion teaches, to serve, to serve everyone else's needs but your own?"

"But how can you give away something you yourself have never possessed?" the therapist asked quietly.

Stephanie shuddered, feeling as if a speeding locomotive was bearing down on her. By denying her permission to choose for herself, her religion had become the substitute for her self, projected out of her own internal void. You actually had to be unworthy in yourself to be worthy of God's love! So if she didn't have a real self, what was it she was giving away to others? How could you give away a you yourself didn't possess? It was like mirrors facing each other, nobodies giving their nobodyness to other nobodies! Oh, God, help me I'm so stupid! she thought. Help me understand! I'm so tired, so tired....

Intuitively, the therapist knew that in that moment, for this client, at this stage of her work, a self was being born.

Not again, but for the first time.

The Master

"Excuse me, master, but I am confused."

The seeker was at that moment doubting his decision to study with this new master. He'd been previously convinced of the completeness of Zen Buddhism as the ultimate philosophy of life, his growing experience in meditation imparting to him a serenity and heart-peace he'd not known possible. But he'd never understand how 'thingness' or the dualism of things could ever arise from the essential 'no-thingness' of Nonduality.

By definition, nonduality couldn't possess any kind of intent to 'make' such thing-ness precipitate, or It Itself would possess dualistic attributes, which was impossible. Furthernore, what was the purpose of nonduality expressing Itself as dualistic separateness in the first place? Zen taught Nonduality was 'not two / not one, but that didn't address why or how 'thing-ness' came to be.

He was also bothered by another question. If the enlightenment experience was access to absolute nondual consciousness, why had no enlightened master ever been conscious of all of the downstream relative measures of finitude in the universe, such as how many gallons of water there were in the oceans or how many trees there were on earth? It seemed reasonable to assume someone who had actually achieved absolute consciousness upstream of all dualisms would 'know' these 'lower' realities from such a 'high' viewpoint.

Not one enlightened master in all of history had ever had that kind of dualistic knowledge imparted to them by their enlightenment. either. So if they didn't, didn't that mean Nonduality Itself, whatever 'It' was, could not be Absolute? And if It was not Absolute, maybe the notion of some mysterious God different than what religion taught was not so far-fetched. Such a God would somehow have to incorporate Nonduality in Its nature and still be responsible for both the creation and the cosmological purpose of dualistic life.

Zen of course never stooped to address questions such as these, considering them to be evidence of the dualistic self still trying to retain itself by insisting things have purpose or make sense. Zen worked fine up until a certain point, but surely some other understanding addressed these kinds of questions. It had been several thousand years since eastern transcendental views had been formulated, and maybe it was time for an update. He committed himself to the quest for that understanding.

He had heard of this new master and only reluctantly became a seeker because of his previous negative experience. But it was said he offered a teaching that was a combination of transcendent Nonduality and devotional experience of Reality, which exactly fit the direction his own path was heading. This community, however, was nothing like the other. This teacher was said to be a true avatar, one who had attained the final wisdom. But at the moment he was having grave doubts as to the accuracy of this conclusion.

"Yes ?" replied the Master.

"I think I have the feeling of what you're saying, but I'm having difficulty with the explanation," he replied. "Isn't it true that self-is-reality, as I have been taught? And that by adherence to the principles of non-ego and the ways of bhakti and dharma, that the wisdom and radiance of Brahman is accessed and expressed through Atman, and thus into the world of dualistic shadow?"

"Undoubtedly," the master replied, amused.

"Then I don't understand what you mean when you say real transcendence includes the transcendence of transcendental effort! These principles are the principles of transcendence. How can you say I must ignore them?"

"I did not say to ignore them. I said to transcend them."

"But how can I transcend the principles that awakened me? Surely you don't imply I return to my former blind state."

"I am suggesting exactly the opposite," replied the master, his smile broadening.

"Then I'm truly at a loss to understand."

"You've done well," the Master replied, in tones of mock gravity, mimicking the seeker's formal seriousness. "You've awakened to the morning rays of the as-yet-unrisen sun that illuminates the far pavilions of life, while the valleys in which you still live remain in darkness." He added earnestly, "Do you wish to remain in these valleys?"

"No! I want to climb that which I can now only view from afar."

"Who wants to climb what?"

The seeker smiled, well versed in the ways of Master-talk. "The I who is not wants to not-climb That Which is not afar."

The Master shook his head sadly, but answered gently, "For the benefit of whom?"

"For the benefit of attaining my own insight, which is the same as benefit to others, as all are one within the Radiant Universal Being."

"According to whose view of the nature of their benefit?"

"Why, mine, of course. Whose view do you follow? If one desires to become a Master, one must cultivate the courage of operating on the nature of his own insight. One can only aid another to the extent of one's own apprehension of reality," the seeker replied, aware of his own growing exasperation.

"Yes," the Master replied, heartily enjoying the devotee's exasperation. "And how does one expand one's apprehension of reality?"

"By embodying the principles I've learned and which you would have me discard!"

"Doesn't each level of understanding or movement serve as compost for the next?" said the Master.

"Yes, of course. But future insight into the nature of reality is included in the transcendental perspective. The very process of transcendence itself creates all of our new vistas of understanding."

"As long as both the process and effects of transcendence are themselves transcended moment-to-moment," replied the Master.

The devotee's mouth opened, but no words would form. He realized that in any interaction of this kind, invariably the one who maintained equanimity while the other agitated embodied the greater wisdom. That he had found himself in the role of the latter frustrated him further, but he had learned well.

He took calmed himself, and focused his mind in mindfulness to lead him to an answer to his confusion. His own integrity required an understanding in harmony with the intuitive grasp, displayed by the consciousness of the master he so deeply wished to emulate. He knew he was not yet so fully realized, but felt in his bones that he was closing in on it and would perhaps achieve it in this life.

The Master followed his thoughts as they paraded across his face. "As always, silence is parent to insight, and grandparent to truth," said the Master jovially. "We'll speak later."

"Wait. Won't you give me something, a direction or idea to meditate upon?"

"No."

"Why not? You lead me to what you think to be a precipice of understanding, which I grant may be what I need, but then you leave me with nothing to pursue.'

"Haven't I? Isn't it your need to pursue something the problem?"

The basic Zen idea of non-attachment, including the attachment to seeking non- attachment, the seeker thought. But I cut my eye teeth on that understanding long ago.

"But doesn't even authentic non-attachment forever contain an unavoidable and subtle attachment, because some one must be always acting to achieve a state of non-action? Musn't there always be a fuel for the fire in which self is immolated, even if it is to be combusted at the moment it becomes operative?" replied the seeker, feeling very clever.

The Master laughed heartily as he rose to leave. "That you may continue to inhere and arise within the Radiant Universal Being does not mean you need to be attached to that truth."

The seeker ached for understanding of how this could possibly be, but could find no solace in the master's response.

Him

"Who are you and what do you want?" the devotee said to the visitor standing in front of her.

The devotee was in no mood for any more surprises. The entire community was edgy due to the master's recent unexplainable distress. For many weeks now, the master had been sequestered, having cancelled his normal schedule and exhibiting a most unenlightened internal self-conflict. This was devastating to his followers, as he was an acknowledged avatar, one who had attained the final wisdom, and so was completely indisposed to self-conflict in any form.

His demeanor had always been one of humor, self-deprecation, and amusement in the absurdity and play of life, He taught that all forms of seeking, eastern meditative as well as western intellectual, were proof of spiritual immaturity. All manner of such self-seeking activity needed to be transcended each moment into the radiance of the transcendental being, until self-conflict, as a subset of the self itself, became impossible.

This development generated two main opinions among the devotees in the small community, the minority maintaining his conduct proved he wasn't avatar after all, while the majority believed this development meant only a new and even more profound insight was emerging in him. This process, although never having displayed this current level of distress, had occurred many times in the past, out of which a new name or title had always accompanied the shift.

As much as she wanted to believe this, the devotee in front of whom this stranger stood remained unconvinced. Having been closest to the master for many years and having spent her former career as a psychotherapist and cult deprogrammer, this recent development filled her with foreboding. She knew absolutely that he was truly enlightened, helping his followers avoid so many blind alleys. So how was she to understand her feeling that something really was wrong, which was impossible from that viewpoint?

She knew him to be human, perhaps the only true example of real humanness on the planet, and had long ago acknowledged within herself personal, unenlightened love for him that included desires of attachment and normal types of possession and clinging. She had resigned herself to this, accepted and not resisted the reality of it so as to be at choice concerning its outward expression, and had spoken often about it with him. She believed this did not affect her judgment concerning this new development, in that if that were so, she would be much more willing to assign new insight emergence to his behavior rather than the feelings she did harbor.

Harbor, she thought. It was an apt metaphor. One harbors one's thoughts when a storm in one's sea of belief is raging.

"I am here to see your master," replied the visitor.

She looked up at him again from behind her glasses, and stared. He was completely unremarkable, displaying no perceptible glow so common in those who had achieved proximity to authentic self-transcendence. But there was something about him that prevented assignation into any specific phase of spiritual development, something her master had taught her to do expertly over the years. A person's affect and bearing gave away volumes of information about where and how self and its ego-signatures still remained. This data defined one's particular degree of advancement along the Path.

To one who'd learned how to see such, people clearly exhibited their particular psychospiritual developmental phase. But for some reason, such a read was not possible with this one. She could not discern anything specific about him except his unshakable and happy confidence. Aside from that, she was aware only of her dizziness, which she attributed to the stress she had been under.

"That's impossible," she said with controlled irritation. "He hasn't allowed anyone audience for weeks," ruefully including herself in that statement. "Who are you? I know everyone here, and visitors make prior arrangements of which only I approve."

"And which you seldom grant."

".... And which I seldom grant, yes. How was it that you were able to get through the gate?"

"It wasn't hard, given the distress everyone is in," he said, with genuine concern. "I promise you, your master needs to see me."

This was ridiculous, she thought. Did he know what had happened to the master? Why was she even considering this, especially with someone not known to her? Her master had specifically and forcefully denied audience to even his closest devotees. At the moment, even she had neither seen nor spoken to him in almost four days, having left his meals outside his quarters. Nothing made any sense anymore. Everything seemed....

"Please," the man insisted gently. "I understand what is happening here. If you love him the way I think you do, you'll let me see him."

The devotee stared at him. The nerve and arrogance of this person! But what was it about him that seemed to him to guarantee her acquiescence? He seemed to be filled with such purposeful momentum that nothing on earth could stop him, unless...unless....he allowed it to, she concluded. Instantly she realized that meant he was allowing her to stop him! He could have walked through her resistance immediately and she wouldn't have been able to stop him. It then occurred to her it had been many years since anyone but her master could cause her to react in such a fashion, as she'd become accustomed to causing this reaction in others.

That realization, combined with his sincerity, concern, and polite appreciation of protocol when such was apparently unnecessary to him, reduced her reservations. Everything was upside down anyway, she thought. The master himself could dismiss this man in a moment if he wanted to, so what was the harm?

She looked up and found him smiling kindly as if he had been following her thoughts completely. "Through there, bear left at the library, and follow the corridor to the stairway. He should be through the first door on your right at the top of the landing, but I can't guarantee it as I've not seen him myself for many days." With that, she could no longer contain her anxiety. Her open, intelligent eyes glistened and flowed, unconcerned a stranger was witness.

The visitor reached over and touched her cheek lightly. "As I'm sure your teacher has said, tears are only condensation on the inner warm side of a window protecting us from some outer cold. As such, they represent our protest against what is, instead of our acceptance of it. If you'll remove the separating glass, your tears will have no surface on which to form, and you can then experience them from a new space that makes it easier to not fuse to the pain. Only then can resolution of the fear, from which the tears flow, begin."

She looked up at him quizzically. That was almost something the master might say, but not quite. Wouldn't he say the fear would end, not begin, when acceptance was ..... .

"Don't worry," the man added gently. "You haven't lost him yet."

She smiled crookedly, trusting him and not understanding why she should. She took his hand and rested her cheek against it, dampening it. "Thank you, whoever you are," she whispered.

He smiled gently in understanding. As he squeezed her hand lightly, he stepped quickly around her desk.

"Who was that?" asked her oldest and closest friend who came up behind her at that moment, the person who'd introduced her to this community. Each knew the other well from the days when both of them were someone else.

"Someone who is not afraid to be alive."

"Not afraid to be alive? What ever do you mean?"

"I don't know," she replied.

Down the corridor in his private quarters, the master lay face down on the floor of his room, sobbing uncontrollably, incapable of any halfway-felt expressions. The dying into each next moment by consciously inhering in the Radiant Universal Being, the predominant expression of his life for many years, had left him only capable of fully experienced existence.

But along with other components of individual selfhood, all elements of his personal emotivity were transcended each moment, all fully arising, fully combusting, and fully dissipating in the blink of an eye. He'd realized life derived all of its purpose and meaning from this continual, moment-to-moment death of self and its desires into the Radiant Universal Being, that seeking of any kind or descent into personal states proved one was still in the throes of seeking for self.

His teachings swept away all of the narcissistically-projected voodoos and superstitions of both exoteric and esoteric spiritual traditions. No master requiring malas, he. He taught relationship with a master was essential to the quickening of transcendental process in the devotee, but that his spiritual maturity and integrity assured that he would be the meal itself in any feast of interaction with a seeker.

But everything changed some weeks ago. A shadow-form, some nexus of congested emotivity, the likes of which he hadn't experienced for almost thirty years, had arisen within the blinding white of his consciousness. Its presence, in the prolonged absence of such phenomena, struck him like a hammer blow to the heart. As with all personally arising emotive states, he attempted to be mindful of it sufficiently to allow it to combust within the now-moment fire of the Transcendental Radiance or to show itself as a transient color forever underlain by Its immovable white wall of featurelessness.

But it would neither incinerate nor cleave itself from That Which Is Eternally, and remained within him as an ever-growing shadow of pain. When he attempted to look at it more investedly to pinpoint its source, it stared back at him in the way that he remembered all internal blind spots do, with a depthless blank. It would not give up its secret, and he had been in abject agony since it arose.

The greater part of his being was still able to be outshined by the Radiant Being of Love-Bliss, but somehow that experience only heightened the hot-point of his pain from this congestion-shadow. He knew there was nothing to pray to for deliverance, that only in the death rattle of merciless mindfulness would he writhe until that part of self containing the fear was outworked and incinerated. He knew from his own experience he couldn't control the length, width, depth, or duration of the process, that he'd endure the pain of it until either he or it no longer existed.

He himself taught it actually didn't matter what the source of the pain was. Fear and pain, no matter its specific content, was incinerated out of one's being by being conscious of the single illusional arisement-point of all individual selfhood moment-to-moment within the Radiant Universal Being. Through the death of the self-context that contained the fear, any vestiges of self-invested fear or conflict were also thus transcended.

But no manner of proximity to the searing transcendental Death / Life-giver seemed to allow transcendence of this emotive congestion. So it remained, burning a deeper and deeper hole in his being, like acid through steel. He felt each molecular dissolution, each atom of his resistance dying in an agony of unrelenting torment. He neither sought the pain nor avoided it. It simply was, and he allowed it to be.

Many a lesser adept would have died long before this, unable to bear an episode of half this intensity. The road to the final knowing was so agonal no one would ever seek It who knew what it entailed. Toward the end, each self-component-held-back-in-fear raged within like an eternally-ricocheting bullet in a closed space, smashing again and again in explosive bursts against the hard surfaces of one's last internal self-invested resistances. Hemorrhage without end, the only clotting mechanism possible being the death of the clotting mechanism itself.

He watched with curious detachment that he was approaching physical death, as almost five weeks of this agony had taken its toll on even his avataric constitution. Somewhere semi-consciously in his being, he was proud he could face the end without giving up the experience of the pain, that it was the enduring of the pain, and not his resistance to It, that would kill him.

His only regret was that this experience proved he had misunderstood something significant, perhaps along the lines of his sexual habits, for which many had criticized him over the years. He knew the price for this. The longer a self-invested delusion remained unaware in one's being, the more terrible the effect of its outworking, the higher the penalty of its unconsciousness upon the consciousness of the experiencer.

That he had remained unaware of it while immolating himself in the Current of Life so completely for so many years thus now actually increased the agony of its outworking effect. The light within had grown so complete that the presence of a darkness now caused intractable pain. But he accepted this nobly, and, like the Zen monk able to drink in the fragile loveliness of a flower before him just prior to his beheading, the master smiled inwardly at the terrible beauty of his own death, unafraid, and, in the central compartment of his being, composed and full of peace.

"Enough."

What was that? Who said that? he thought. Through the milky opacity of his agony he looked up to see a man with his hands in his pockets standing easily in the open doorway of his quarters. He then became aware this person had been standing there for some time. He was inclined to ignore him, but was shocked at his awareness of a feeling of impertinence at the intrusion. Despite his current state, he remained sufficiently clear to realize this could only mean his own suffering and death held enough self-importance to him to not wish another to witness it. This was not something that could be tolerated. He couldn't allow any manner of self-importance within his being.

It was this realization that forced him, in an effort only knowable to others who have endured even a small portion of that death-process, to gather up his pain, compartmentalize it, and stand shakily to face this man who had without effort caused him to come in contact with this awareness. That he was able to do so in a matter of moments was proof of his avataric nature.

"Your own integrity kills you," said the man.

The master was somehow not surprised at the accuracy of that statement, even though the man was a stranger to him. "There is a preferable angel of death?" the master replied shakily.

"Why, yes," said the man easily, smiling. "Something other than the arrogance contained in the belief that your own integrity has a right to kill you."

The master immediately captured the import of the man's words and sagged badly. Only the lightning movement of the man saved him from collapsing face first onto the hard floor.

After some minutes of unconsciousness, the master awoke to find the man sitting on the floor in the middle of the room, himself lying in his arms, being held gently. In his embrace, the master found surcease from his pain for the first time since its unwelcome arrival. The absolute outrageousness of this interaction with a stranger was not lost to him, but that did not detract at all from his ability to drink thirstily from the fullness of the moment.

"You knew I felt presumptuousness at your intrusion?"

"Of course," replied the man. "The root of that is the root of the shadow that kills you."

"Which is what?"

"The same basis for your habit of keeping devotees, having sex with them, and changing your name every time you have a new insight. It exposes the undeniable fact that a part of you still finds it necessary to need both devotion by others and to strategically manipulate symbological reality to create an effect. You do these things in order to make yourself not feel the fear remaining in you and thus to avoid a fundamental error of your teaching."

"Which error?"

"The mistaken belief that even an authentic process of self-transcendence results in the resolution and release of our pain and fear."

The master considered this. Wasn't the individual self really just a fear-contraction itself within the Radiance of the Universal Being? If one burns a box with an object in it, and the object arises from and is made of the same material as the box, when the box is ashes, so must be the object. So if fear resided within the self, and the dualistic self was thus transcended, so must the fear contained within it.

"No," said the man, responding to his unspoken thoughts. "And all the unconscious fears remaining in you that never rose to be considered and are never transcendable even if they did, have prevented you from encountering the Maker of all things, with Whom we all need to inhabit personal connect no matter how advanced we become. After enlightenment, only countenance with It allows all of our pious or enlightened arrogances to be washed away."

The master's mind cleared and reached for understanding that would explain the words the man used, but he struck his internal head hard against something within him that felt like a wall of sheer rock. He reeled dizzily from the collision.

"Easy, easy," said the man, stroking the master's forehead and following his internal process easily. "There'll be enough of that later. For now, rest."

The devotee who had let the man in found them in that position, as she, unable to not be witness to an interaction between these two men, stood aghast in the doorway of the master's quarters.

Mar-yam

The first thing she experienced as she slowly awakened was the echo of the steady rain against the walls of the grotto. She was surprised to find her cheeks wet with tears. For a moment she couldn't feel the difference between the feeling of the rain outside and the feeling inside her that brought the tears, as if tears and rain were different expressions of the same emotion.

She had often heard spoken the poetic linkage between the two, but had never felt the inner truth of that so deeply. She often awoke recently with tears flowing from some unknown piercing in the night, and knew they portended a difficult day ahead. Mar-Yam of Migdal, now of Gaul, huddled more deeply into her bed of straw.

The morning was cold, and as the familiar sights, sounds, and smells of the cave she'd called home for so many years entered her, she was glad for the small comfort. She lay under a colorful woven blanket made for her by her friend Mira of Galilee, who had spent almost a year creating it. Mar-Yam could always detect the faint smell of Mira's favorite nard in the blanket. But this morning, intensified by the dampness on the grotto, the aroma was intense and flooded her with feelings of both love and loss, intertwined as tightly as the strands of the blanket that warmed her.

Oh, Mira, she thought .... so many unshared heartbeats lay between us after so much time. Did you still have the hourglass I gave you when I left, the one filled with the sand of the Negev, from where I spent so much time with my beloved, the one that takes a whole month to complete its cycle? Do you think of me when you see the sand falling through the narrow channel, each grain a reminder of how many moments our love for each other falls through time?

We knew when we met as children we were sisters of different mothers. We both knew the language of silence and how it let us hear the voices of the blossoms and the clouds. Do you remember the day we ran out into the rain so we could dance with it as it soaked our robes, and how we could hear the song of the rainbow it created that day? Will you ever forget the sad day we realized what the shrikes did, impale uneaten parts of the birds they captured onto the thorn bushes, how we felt about that, and struggled to understand it?

Do you remember how hard it was to only see you once a year after your first red days and you were confined to the hidden temple to be groomed as the head priestess? Did you feel me feel your pain about how that meant you would never be with a man as beloved this life? That you were chosen and then chose to serve men that other way, the way I could never abide, meant that our lives had to cleave?

I could never understand how taking men to God through the body that way liberated anything, least of all women. I know you felt judged by me for this, but I knew you knew I could never stop loving you. I valued so much all that you taught me in the other arts of perceptual nuance, connection with all that is, and reading the ethers for intuitive knowledge.

I missed you so much that day in Cana when Yeshua and I married. I know you sent the lovely flowers and the wonderful ointments, but nothing could replace your living presence and how it always made me feel. Yeshua felt it also, and I think he loved you more than he ever said. I pray with all my heart that in the next life you give yourself the gift of one man as beloved. Even with all the capacity for the dream with a man to become a nightmare, it is worth it. To be with a man that way doesn't mean we are not with ourselves or with God: I know this in my heart but have struggled to find the words for it. I so wanted you to know this also, and let it be a binding between us.

I still ache that you would not come with me here to Gaul after all that happened. I know you said you could not leave your own destiny path, and in that way you and Yeshua were so alike, so different than me. You both could always seem to easily leave the personal behind in service to your spiritual paths. I often thought that you two were soulmates in that one way. But why must the personal and the universal be enemies instead of kindred spirits? Why do I feel the war between them taught to us by all the prophets is wrong?

Why is it so hard for me to walk away from the personal? Is it because I lack some intrinsic trait, or is it because I possess something neither of you two do? So if it is an absence, is that a good or bad thing? And if it is a presence, is that a good or bad thing? No matter how deeply I scour the bottom of my own heart and implore my Maker for guidance in this, I can find no answer. Am I just too stubborn or too strong? Am I farther away from gnosis as you two seem to hold, or closer than both of you?

And why is it so easy for men to deny the mind when they live so deeply in it? Why did Master Gotama abandon his wife and child, and why did you do the same, my beloved? Did you want to be like him, leave all personal attachments behind in order to please our Maker? What about what the heart is crying to say? Does personally binding to another in love always mean over-attachment? Maybe both you and Master Gotama were both just afraid that loving your woman and child meant you could not fulfill your spiritual destinies. If that is so, isn't that the very selfishness you say you are avoiding by leaving us? Maybe you both were just afraid to be men.

Mar-Yam sighed deeply. In the end, we are not defined by men, dear Mira, even though both men and women are taught this. We are born to dance with them, yes, but not to be defined by them. It is even not as the Essenes say, that there is only one woman in the world but that she has many faces. The Essenes feel they honor women in that universal way, but how could they not see that that diminishes us horribly, and disallows the sovereign sense of our personal nature?

This is why Yeshua and I both knew that neither the Essenes' teaching nor the Law of Moses was complete, that neither Essenic gnosis nor Judaic heaven represented the true destination of the soul. Something has always been missing, and what is missing somehow involves what men have always missed about the nature of woman as they have taught us about God.

Women also come with a destiny. We too come to bring God to earth, but in a different way than men. Why is there not room for us in God's Plan other than servant to men? Where is the space for us to create our own tapestry of heart and soul, vibrating in different but equal gifts of being as men? To find my love with a man like Yeshua who understood the heart of women and supported me so much, was a bestowal beyond words. That he was this way with me this in spite of the opposition of so many of the disciples, especially Peter, engraved him into my heart in a way that can never be erased.

To be blamed by Peter in the end for all the chaos that happened was the poison on the knife-tip, the final insult against me for daring to not to be a slave. As I got older, I realized that most men are like the shrikes: after they have used women, they leave the uneaten portions on the thorns of a woman's own feminine agony. How can they not hear our cries, silent as they are, but as such because no one will listen? Yeshua always could. That is how I knew he was my man. He showed me that to be man did not mean to be cut off from heart. But that made it so much harder to understand what he did in the end.

Yeshua, my beloved …. where are you this moment? Are you safe in your world in the east after fleeing Judea and how close you came to dying at Golgoth? Do you still think of me when you look at the sunset, even after all these years? Do the stars still transport the voice of our eternal bond? Do you look at the moon and feel me as I am and always will be? Do you still feel the soft imprint in your soul that my soul made in yours, as I always feel yours in mine? Does the song of the starling still stir your loins as it does mine? Do the change of the seasons remind you how our yin and yang danced? Or has time slowly filled that living conduit between us with the dust of acceptance, the acceptance you allowed to justify your decision to leave?

How can I love you after all this time after how you broke my heart? How can I hate you as much as I love you? How many more prayers must I make before Maker forgives me my selfishness and my certainty that I was right and you were wrong?

Did you know our child had died so young? Can you feel how she felt all of my pain and so could not live long, weakened by it and thus easily overtaken by sickness? I buried her in Les Baux with our bonded dream of being, my beloved. And without our dream of bonded being, life for me is a daily torture even after all these years.

I hate my memory, she thought. Just as the ocean has no memory, its movement and waves eternal and never alike one moment to the next, I want to be a sea of forgetfulness as the Master Gotama taught. To have the past be only a dream and the future an illusion, as Life bubbles up in its unexpected ways in the now and taking us with It to destinations we cannot imagine, create, or prevent. You were always better at that than me, she thought. But why have I always felt that was both a strength and a weakness in you? And if I feel that it might be also weakness, why do I also seek that release so deeply?

She closed her eyes tightly, summoning a picture of Yeshua's gray eyes and how they looked the last time she saw him, as he began his journey alone after he had healed from the debacle of the crucifixion, for which he had only himself to blame. Has it been worth it, my love? Have you found your expiation for causing so much heartache and pain to all of us by your actions? Have you healed yourself of the shame of setting events into motion to cause your brother Judas to leap from that cliff, he then also abandoning his wife and child?

How was abandoning Sarah and I the answer to what you did? Why must more hearts be shattered and dreams rotted to pay for how you betrayed your own countenance with our Maker? Why is it the women and children always suffer for the actions of man? Why does our humanness have to be denied to enlighten our divinity? Why do we have a human heart if it is only meant to be torn to bits in service of our breath of universal spirit?

How can I ever find my own countenance with Divine Being if I am bedeviled by such doubts? she thought to herself, wiping the tears away with the edge of the blanket. I came here thirteen years ago to find that deliverance. Why has it not found me? Day after day, week after week, month after month, year after year of solitude, prayer, fasting, and meditation? Why can't my heart burst once and for all into the Greater Good of God, from whence we all emanate? Why is there no relief of my personal pain? Do I need it too much or am I too strong to knowingly abandon it?

Mar-Yam turned on her right side, hearing the incessant drip of the cistern in the far corner of her stony home. That is my hourglass, she thought. That is my reckoning of time. How many drops since I came here after Sarah died? I can't tell if each drop marks the passing of me or the birth of me each moment. I remember when the four of us first arrived, me, Joseph Arimethea, the dark-skinned handmaiden we brought from Egypt, and John.

As the hidden leader of the Essenes, Joseph had arranged passage to Gaul, all of us cramped in that small boat, I with child and only with the grace of God not capsized those many times. How grateful I was when we arrived on that beach, and made so happy by how the Gallic Essenes had welcomed us, and how for almost five years things were as well as could be expected. I tried to teach what we both taught in Judea, but without your yang, my yin was only half the story. We both knew the time had come for both a man and a woman to teach God together and move Spirit away from yang-only expressions. Now that dream is only smoke in the wind, left to another lifetime.

When Sarah died, the last part of my strength to bear everything was lost. How do you lose your soul beloved and your child both in one life and still remain alive in heart? Just accept the pain, give to our Maker, and try to forget? Is that being human? What else could I do but seek the grotto here in the solitude, a place where I could spend the rest of my days seeking my Maker in the way you know It, and with that to finally know the meaning and the purpose of my life and in the end, the one form of gnosis that would release me.

Looks like it will rain all day today, she thought. Best I rise and get the fire going. John will be bringing me my monthly supplies later in the day from Nams-les-Pins. She thought, I know John loves me and vowed to serve that love in this way for as long as he lived, but I hurt him so much in my unreturned feelings. How is it good for him to keep serving someone who loves him only as friend and not beloved?

And so begins another day, another ten thousand drops of the cistern, another arc of a hidden sun refusing to gift me with its warmth, another challenge to rise to life and ask it to show me why I should continue to live it. I am happy in one way that I know this grotto will soon be my tomb as it has also been this last part of my life. She rose then and moved to the east wall of the grotto, knelt on the flat stone placed there for that purpose, and said her daily prayer of awakening, the one that she and Yeshua used to pray together at the beginning of every day they spent with each other:

'Oh my Maker
let all turn aflame
that the sifting of my ashes
yields the indestructible.'

That day, for the first time, she realized that she had neither expected the flames to be so painfully long-lasting, nor the emergence of the indestructible so elusive.

It

Who speaks in my name?

A world that wishes upon a star

but breathes dizzily only in broken dreams

fearful to roll back its own stubborn stone

behind which

I

have

always

lain

awaiting only the crucifixion of fear

and the resurrection of Love

that the one within All

the All within None

and the None within Me

today awakens

to the sun and moon

of a layered lived-in Life

Paradigms on Parade

"Hello everyone! Welcome to Paradigms on Parade! The only show in television where world-views are explicated, value systems are vindicated, and belief systems are lubricated! I'm Jake P. Whittle, and tonight we have a show that has literally been over two thousand years in the making!"

"After long negotiation, patient prevarication, and their agents' amelioration, tonight's guests come to us from all corners of the globe and from all niches in history. Tonight, for your educational edification, rapacious reification, and pious pontification, from India please welcome Prince Siddhartha, a.k.a. the Buddha; from Israel, Yeshua of Judea, a.k.a. Jesus of Nazareth; and hailing from both Russia and the Big Apple, Alissa Zinovievna Rosenbaum, a.k.a. Ayn Rand!"

All three guests bowed from their seats as the audience applauded raucously. Rand was dressed fashionably in black Armani, Yeshua humbly clad in an off-white seamless one-piece chiton woven from Argenteuil cloth, and Buddha in a striking cotton homespun robe dyed in the deep oranges and reds of the Delhi sunset.

Whittle continued, "Tonight's illustrious guests were distilled from a list of many religious, spiritual, and philosophical leaders past and present because of their archetypal paradigmatic offerings for their specific, singular, and completely antithetical positions about the nature of individual human selfhood. Because of this, their followers in the audience have been duly constrained from crossing into each other's seating areas in order to minimize any unpleasantness. And Evangelicals and Catholics in the Christian section, please respect the red velvet roping separating your areas."

Whittle wiped his brow, grateful to get the show started after the Muslim picketers outside the front of the studio protesting the omission of Muhammed from the show had threatened to bomb the building if their demand that the Prophet be included was not met. Pleading by the show's producers that Muhammed had never offered

135

a definitive and discreet paradigmatically-specific position on the nature of human selfhood, had fallen on the local imam's deaf ears, who then issued a fatwa about the apostasy of infidels and called for immediate action against both the studio and its sponsoring network.

A SWAT team with explosive-sniffing dogs had been brought in to search the building and found nothing, but it had delayed the show's taping for over two hours. Whittle knew the vast majority of Muslims were peaceful sweet people, albeit stuck in a religious collectivistic paradigm from the past, and had many Muslim friends who were as shocked as the rest of the world at the actions of a small but deadly percentage of radicals who interpreted the Q'uran to fit their own destructive political ideology.

At least the celebrity seating arrangements had mostly gone well. Meister Eckhart, Yogananda, and Mohandas Gandhi had arrived together and graciously took their appropriate seats on the far side of the stage. Zororaster, Abraham, and Moses did likewise. Confucius and Lao-Tse were at a conference in Tibet, which was a relief. Jake was afraid they might take advantage of the TV audience to make some high profile politicking against Red China.

But Deepak Chopra was so upset in being unsuccessful in his attempt to persuade the producers to let him replace Jake as a guest host for this particular show, that he stalked off and said he couldn't predict what kind of earthquake might happen around the studio if he were to begin meditating upon Shiva.

Oprah was also so dismayed that Paradigms on Parade would likely outsell her own show for record advertising revenue, that she took her entire studio audience to Papua, New Guinea along with Eckhart Tolle, and promised everyone a free personalized mantra.

And Nathaniel Brandon, when denied an equal stage seating with Ms. Rand, declared that his books had ideas she hadn't thought of, and that he should be as recognized as much as she in the application of Objectivismic principles and expressions. Alan Greenspan, formerly of the Federal Reserve, had been present in the studio then and almost came to physical blows with Brandon. Jake had to separate the two senior citizens from actually punching each other out.

Ah, well.....Jake exhaled. Given the time and effort that went into getting these three guests, all in all it had proceeded smoothly enough. He then consciously re-acquired his upbeat stage persona, took a deep breath and shouted to the audience, "All right everyone, can we please hear from those hailing for Ms. Rand?"

Rand's section, having the fewest numbers, nonetheless let out with a loud, wet, and noisy Bronx cheer, in exquisite and deliberate irony. "Wonderful! Classy cacophony, Randers! Gutsy Galt's Gulchers nonverbally nuancing! And now, for Yeshua of Judea?"

The entire Christian section stood up, and began to jump up and down in almost a trance-like frenzy cheering, raising their arms, stamping their feet, with the Catholics genuflecting in the aisles of their section and the Evangelicals repeating the chant: 'What-would-Jesus-do? I know!-What-would-Jesus-do? I know!'

Whittle gave them the thumb's up. "Hallelujah, Christophiles! The Lord loves ya! May the rapture redeem you, the pope esteem you, and no atheist demean you! And for Prince Siddhartha?"

There was only silence in response, as all the members of the Buddhist section sat quietly cross-legged with their eyes half-open, possessed of enigmatic half-smiles, and with all their forefingers touching their thumbs.

"Namaste, navel-divers! Perfectly imperfect! Chop that wood and carry that water!" Whittle exulted and turned to the camera. "Tonight's show begins with each guest getting three minutes to state their primary thesis of the nature of individual human selfhood, then extend that thesis by describing their position concerning the cause of human suffering, its cure, and finally, offering a description of the highest state of human consciousness as taught by their paradigm!"

"Go Jesus go! You da son of God!" cried one from the Christian section. "Show 'em who's bodhisattva!" cried the current Dala'i Lama from the Buddhist section. "Annihilate the altruists!" a brave member from the Randian section yelled, as others in his section reacted disdainfully, embarrassed by his gauche obviousness.

"Who would like to start us off?" Whittle asked.

"I will," said Rand. "And that is exactly it," she said, turning to the camera. "The 'will' of the 'I' is the starting point of everything." The Randians in the audience murmured self-satisfyingly, the Buddhists shook their heads ruefully but acceptingly, and the Christians scowled menacingly, whispering to each other.

Rand continued, "Individual human selfhood, a by-product of our essential physical nature as sentient animals and sourced solely by the brain and nervous system, is the fountainhead for all that is good in this world, the pivotal dynamism for all human achievement and evolution, and the only fuel-source for humanistic-based meaningfulness and clarity in relationship with all others."

"The unapologetic embracement of human happiness is the only reasonable goal of life, and the means to attain that is the dedication to the best within us as we refuse to sell out self's truth for the maundering service to others, while we produce creative expressions of selfhood and refuse to ever be a second-hander or looter of other's product of effort in any entitled way."

She took a breath and continued, "The cause of all human suffering is the religio-mystical proscription of a self's right to its own sovereignty, dominion, and joy, where altruism is the poison that purports to bring the end of suffering when it is a primary cause of it. The cure for human suffering lies in intellectualized values clarification in the context of the abject rejection of all mystical world-views and values that deny the self's right to exist and thrive, with no apology for the wealth earned as the appropriate reward for one's commitment to self and its productive expression."

"And last, the highest state of human consciousness is that of one who will not yield, will not give up, and will not allow their values to be distilled by the bromides of history's promenade of self-stagnative and self-destructive paradigms such as those created by the two anti-self non-persons who sit at this very table."

"You're going to hell for insulting my Jesus like that!" an angry Evangelical Christian shouted bitterly from the audience.

"What do you care?" replied Rand, amused. "If I am going to hell, that is my problem, not yours. Why should it concern you in such a vituperative way? If you were sure of your paradigm, wouldn't you be smiling and happy as you say that to me, because I would then be getting what you say I so rightly deserve, according to your paradigm? Doesn't being angry with anyone who disagrees with you, show you are actually and unconsciously unsure about what you say you believe, because if you really believed it in this case, you would be happy and not angry about me going to hell?"

The Evangelical looked dazed and confused, his consciousness quotient seriously exposed in that moment. "Oh....um....well, I just...."

"The prosecution rests," answered Rand, shaking her head and relishing the moment. "Any religion that responds with anger or violence to anyone who disagrees with them completely proves they are actually unsure of their religion. Someone who was sure of their religion would just shrug off those they deemed heretic because they would 'know' it was wrong anyway according to their world-view, so why be bothered by it?"

She continued, "They would not only not be angry, if they actually followed what they say they believe in, they would be forgiving and compassionate about the 'poor lost souls' who had not yet embraced the 'truth,' and not be made angry or do violence to them in their 'ignorance,' seeing them all as children of God or Allah who need their help, and not any self-righteous punishment."

Rand rose from her chair and added passionately, "By responding with bitterness, rage, or violence to anyone who disagrees with a religion's position, that religion reveals in that moment how they are not only not clear and not sure about what they hold as the content of their own metaphysics, it directly goes against what it teaches and so dishonors the very God or Allah it says the religion represents!"

The Randians stood up and hooted triumphantly, this time non-ironically, while the Buddhists again shook their heads and smiled knowingly. The pope in the Catholic section looked extremely nervous as he began pulling out the overgrowth of untrimmed hair in his ears. And the picketing Muslims watching the taping on a big screen outside on the street responded to Rand by shouting and thrusting their fists in the air, screaming, "Ji-had! Ji-had! Ji-had! The whore has insulted the Prophet! Death-to-all-infidels! Allahu Akbar Allahu! Allahu Akbar Allahu!"

"Thank you, Ms. Rand," Whittle responded back in the studio. "An unequivocal paradigmatic assertion, delivered with just the right combination of subtle disdain, intellectual depth, and deeply incisive metaphysical clarity." He paused, and then said to the Buddha and Yeshua, "Which of you would like to go next?"

"I'll speak," said Yeshua, as the Buddha nodded in agreement. "But first I need to clear up that no matter what the Council at Nicea thought it was doing, I had a human mother and father, married Mar-Yam of Migdal, the thirteenth apostle, did not die at Golgoth, did not rise from the dead, and with Mar-Yam had a girl-child Sarah who died in early childhood. The Gospels were retro-edited to push the Jesus-as-God party line decided upon by Constantine to unify his empire with one overall religion. I actually died alone as an old man, teaching my truths in India."

The Evangelicals were dumbstruck for a few seconds, then began screaming and tearing at their clothes. The rabbi from Brooklyn sitting with his friend the American cardinal in the Catholic section smiled in satisfaction, while the pope took a break from pulling out his ear hair, stood up and yelled, "Imposter! Imposter! This is Satan pretending to be our Savior!" and began crossing himself.

Yeshua looked up at him quizzically and said, "Excuse me, but do I know you? Who are you and why are you dressed like that?"

Whittle intervened, "Thank you, Yeshua, for the clarifications that many of us have held as true all along, without rejecting the basic themes of your singular and compelling message of Love. Dan Brown and Ron Howard will certainly be happy tonight! Can we get you to make your opening statement please?"

"Yes, thank you, Jake," Yeshua replied, turning away from the pope. "We are all children of a Loving God, and our legacy in spirit manifesting as what we call human selfhood, the soul expressing in flesh. Our soul-consciousness as the body is mediated through the brain as a physically grounding receiver, compiler, editor, and expressor of soul-stream frequencies of being. We are in earth to make choices in alignment with our heritage of Spirit and to learn to love ourselves equally as we love our neighbors, not love neighbors more, as usually and incorrectly practiced."

"The cause of human suffering is thus the indifference to the ramifications of our Source in God, as we project the devils of our own unrevealed spirithood onto ourselves and out onto others and thus fight both, disregarding the Love of which we are all made. In that way, there is no Satan other than our own Will that puts itself ahead of Love. The Creator is Love, nothing else, and the vengeance and wrath projected upon Him by confused humans and religions are woefully misguided and not at all what He is."

"Almost all human suffering is thus caused by putting our personal Will first and Love second, reversing the actual architecture of our beings. Each of us is in essence Love incarnate, given free will by our Parent to secondarily move our deeper natures through the Love that is God. As such, we have never needed any scripture, clergy, or middle-man religion to re-ligate our connection with our Loving Father. All religion is made up by human beings, with none of them any righter or wronger than another, all the while our Creator patiently awaits us to find Him within and through the fabric of our human lives, relating to Him directly as the context for all of our choices."

"The cure for human suffering is thus that in any one life we choose, through prayer and surrender of our will to the Will of God and connecting our essential Love-being in alignment with the Love-Being of God, to live a life starting with Love, moving that Love through Will secondarily and becoming in that way a beacon of Love and Light in a dark world where Will has been embodied as prior to Love, overshadowing the essence of our own nature in that way, and thus screening from us that this earth was created by God as the waking heaven of our dreams, where angels and humans co-inhabit in nature, at peace with themselves and with all living things."

"The penultimate state of human development is thus the duplication of my consciousness-being of Love as I live and embody these truths, and not by adoringly making a God out of me, which only keeps me above and all others below. As such, you create a vibrational central frequency of soul that resonates with our Father that will change the very frequencies of your cells as a human being with a body. This makes your soulful alignment now in body and later in the afterlife with our Source, not as an attainment you seek, but an embodiment you become, of That Which we've always been made: Love."

Many of the Christian section had walked out grumbling after the comments about no need for any religion, scripture or clergy, and many of those who stayed behind had fainted in the aisles. The rabbi had leaned over to his friend the cardinal and said, "Guess you'll have to find a new line of work, yes?" The pope had sat back down, unable to move, and resumed his pulling the hair in his ears.

Whittle asked, "Yeshua, did I hear you say something about 'in any one life?' Are you saying you taught that re-incarnation was real?"

"Yes, of course I did," Yeshua responded. "What kind of just and merciful God would mandate we learn all these amazingly difficult truths about Love, Will, Freedom, and Choice only in one life, when we are so badly damaged and conditioned by our families and our societies? You can actually remember your past lives yourself if you train your consciousness to change the way it focuses on things."

He took a breath and added, "The Essenes, who helped train me, knew about re-incarnation and saw it as a natural path to learning to become conscious children of God. My teaching about it was dropped out and considered heretical after Nicea, along with most of the heart of my teaching. What was left as the foundation for a new religion should have been called Paulianity, because it was his mistaken interpretation of my teaching that became codified as Christianity."

He shook his head. "I taught self-redemption, with no one to save you but yourself. Paul never got that, and incepted a religion whose abidance and arrogance will obscure and not access, the true nature of God. You can never abide with the living God while only believing in Him in the ways all the religions promote."

Yogananda and Gandhi jumped up and hollered in support, while Meister Eckhart smiled from his seat. Zororaster, Abraham, and Moses clapped politely but frowned from their seats. Whittle stood amazed. "You heard it here first, folks! Yeshua of Judea saying re-incarnation was part of his original teaching, he never died on the cross to save humanity, you don't need religion or any kind of scripture to find God, and that Christianity in all its forms does not represent his actual teaching! Holy Hallelujah, this changes everything!"

Even more Christians exited from the studio after this, leaving only a handful pondering the ramifications of this entirely new way of what Yeshua had taught. Even the Randians were strangely silent, although they scoffed about the soul sourcing the brain. The Buddhists heartily applauded the item about re-incarnation, with the Dala'i Lama laughing hysterically, like a donkey braying.

Whittle turned to the Buddha, and said, "This admission by Yeshua about re-incarnation must be a huge vindication for you, Prince Siddhartha."

"It does no such thing, Jake," replied the Buddha, kindly but assertively. "Contrary to mass consciousness forms of Buddhism, I taught that here is no such thing as re-incarnation because there is no self, no nothing in what we call a human being to re-incarnate."

He paused, then continued. "The self is not something to extinguish, it is something that never existed in the first place! All that bodhisattva and transmigration of soul teaching is just old folklore of Hinduism improperly grafted onto my teaching over the centuries by confused followers unable to grasp the truth of what I taught. Nirvana is not some kind of unitive paradise: it is the utter negation of any Thing that thinks it is some Thing, that at the root of all illusory Things is That Which is beyond Thing-dom of all kinds, That Which is utterly unexperiencable by the mind-created illusory self."

The Dala'i Lama stopped laughing, sat down, closed his eyes, and began chanting 'Nam-myoho-renge-kyo' over and over again. The rest of the Buddhists went uncharacteristically noisy as they began what looked like grooming each other, as monkeys do when they search for bugs in each other's fur, distracting themselves that way from what had just been said. Whittle noticed the disquiet in the audience, and said, "We're getting a little ahead of ourselves here, folks. Siddhartha, would you please formally make your statement?"

"Of course." Siddhartha's tones and demeanor were soft and warm, but his words arose like bullets of clarity. "What we call human selfhood is nothing but a co-arising between external phenomena and stimuli and the bodymind's nervous system. The bodymind responds to dualistic experience, registers that experience in the brain, and stores it in what we call memory."

"The way the brain stores experience as memory thus makes it seem as if there is then some kind of un-changing selfhood sourcing experience, when the truth is that ever-changing experience is what not only originally sourced the perception of an un-changing self, it accounts for its ongoing seemingly solid buoyancy, which in essence actually is as ever-changing as the experience that created it."

General uneasy murmuring continued in the Buddhist section, while the Christians and Catholics had a general 'Huh?' on their faces. Most of the Randers were yawning, but the men who weren't were busily looking over the women in their section. Seeing themselves as a Roark or a Galt, they were looking for a sexual conquest with a female who saw herself as a Dominique or a Dagny.

Siddhartha continued, "The cause of all human suffering is the attachment to the attraction/repulsion dualistic dynamic that wholly comprises what we call selfhood and our emotively-suffused reaction to experience, caused only by the way the dualistic mind cuts up and experiences experience. Attachment to the attraction/repulsion reactions to phenomena thus imparts an illusory sense of self, and further deeper attachment to that illusory selfhood reduces human life into positions and polarizations of right/wrong, true/false, and this/that dynamics that are at root the cause of all of our pain and travail."

"The cure for human suffering is the realization that such an illusory sense of solid selfhood is a complete fabrication of the mind, allowed by the gradual de-dualization of the bodymind through meditation and specific kinds of ruthless self-inquiry to undermine the attachment to our illusory nature."

"This de-dualizational dharma eventually causes the emotive attraction/repulsion dynamic to loosen as the dualistic mind that contains it is transcended. This causes the illusory self to fall away, and the resultant base-lining of consciousness then imparted by That Which allows all perception to arise, blossom, and dissipate, destroys all attachments to preferential outcomes of life, and creates an inner serenity and peaceable nonreactivity to all experience."

"In that way, human suffering is eliminated into and inheres as That Which Is beyond anything the mind can experience, and is subsequently lived as the primary modality of consciousness, with all secondary experience as passing impermanence."

"The ultimate state of self consciousness is thus a not-state of not-consciousness, no self, no God, no afterlife, no inherent meaning to human life, no immortality project of any kind whatsoever. The religions and philosophies of the world thus offer nothing more than attachments to childish or teenage fairy tales. They all argue the merit of their pet understandings as they are held in the content of dualistic allegorical positions about reality. What is needed is to move beyond all such allegorical positions about reality to the context of That Which is Reality, That Which holds all content of all kinds within Its Transcendental Be-ing equally, like the stewpot that holds the rice."

He smiled and added, "The Truth is thus never found in which bit of rice is 'right,' but in That Which all riceness wholly inheres within.

In that way what I teach is not a paradigm at all, but is That Which is beyond all paradigms of all kinds, and thus the only true Absolute."

Whittle smiled ingratiatingly. "Thank you, Siddhartha. We will all need some time to digest that. For now though, can you please answer the one question that has burned in the minds of seekers for millennia? After enlightenment, who or what still retains whatever kind of not-self consciousness arises in relational space? If Nonduality is beyond all identity, who or what is talking when an enlightened teacher or master speaks?"

The Buddha smiled compassionately. "The answer is in the question! As you say, the question itself lies in the mind of the seeker. The answer cannot be found in the mind of the seeker because it is in the mind that all limits arise! Only in the not-mind of the finder can the answer be found. There can never be any real answer to any question that still lives in the mind. And that truth is something which you can only know as true after enlightenment."

"But then how would the not-mind of an enlightened finder actually answer that question?" Jake pressed.

Siddhartha replied, "They would say, 'Any question posited for a definitive answer that disallowed any other answer, can only be about reality, and not inhere as reality. Real coherence can inhere, but real inherence does not necessarily cohere in ways an unenlightened mind might prefer."

"OK, wow, that's challenging, thank you," replied Whittle. "I don't get it, *but I guess that's the point!*" Turning to the camera, he said, "So there you have it folks, three completely contradictory paradigms or world-views, each having a deep effect on our evolution as a species, each with their own......."

"They are not contradictory." A man who had been standing quietly in the back of the studio audience had spoken. His voice was both strong and kind.

"Excuse me ....?" said Whittle, looking him over. "Sir, we have just heard three antithetical world-views from their original founders that completely disagree about the base definition of human selfhood, the cause and cure of human suffering, and the ultimate state of consciousness available to human beings. How can you say they are not contradictory?"

"Because they all possess some aspect of truth while all possessing deeply erroneous assumptions about human essence that undermine their legitimacy, and make each of them no longer apply to this stage of human evolution of consciousness."

Whittle smiled as he smelled controversy, always good for the ratings. To the camera he said, "So our audience member here claims to have more insight than Ms. Rand, Yeshua, and the Buddha put together, is that right, sir?"

The man smiled kindly. "Not more. Just different."

Whittle scoffed and said, "So will you expound upon your thesis for us all?"

The man considered this. "No," he said. "I'll show you instead."

A woman from the Rand section yelled out in laughing tones, "So, what .... are you saying you are, like, the 'One,' Neo from The Matrix?"

"No," replied the man, smiling. "But in that metaphor, your worldview represents the machines' mind-only primacy of reality. The 'One' is not me, but What I represent."

"And how will you show us, and what do think you represent?" asked Ms. Rand, confident and superior, even without her cigarettes.

The man seemed amused and looked directly at her, his eyes boring into hers. "I don't 'think' it: I feel it. You smugly think you own the rights to define what is essentially human, but you missed the most foundational element. And I will show you what I represent, what you missed, and how much you still have to learn, by stopping the paradigmatic motor of the world."

Rand felt immediately riveted to her seat. 'Wait a minute,' she thought to herself. 'He can't take my ....' Then she realized that this man was holding far more power toward her than she was able to hold toward him. Her breath caught in her throat, her eyes narrowed, and she thought, 'Must have .... him .... I must .... .'

Yeshua intervened kindly just then and said, "And how will you do that, my bold and heartful brother?"

The man smiled at Yeshua. "By showing, with the help of our Maker, that you, Yeshua, found a way to encounter the ultimate Yang Aspect of Divine Being and built a world-view upon that attainment; and how you, Siddhartha, found a way to encounter the ultimate Yin Aspect of Divine Being and built a world-view upon that, even though you deny it is a world-view; and how you, Alissa, found one or two ways to describe the human Child Aspect of Divine Being sourced by both the Yang and Yin of Divine Being, and built your compelling but incomplete philosophy upon that."

"But what kind of overarching paradigm would impart such a conciliatory view, in such a way as to redefine all of what these great teachers say?" asked Whittle.

The man smiled again, but not a happy one. In sad tones, he said, "Exactly the right question, Jake. We'll have to talk more about it later. Suffice it to say all three of them have always missed something about our humanity that has always been right under our paradigmatic noses, the awareness of which would change almost everything about how they hold their truths." He spoke to the audience and said, "Thank you all for a very illuminating day."

He then turned to a woman who had been standing to his left and said, "Shall we?" as he extended his arm. With that, she smiled up at him, took his arm, and together they walked without any rush out of the studio, calmly past all the shouting Muslims on the street, and anonymously into the streets of Manhattan.

There was a quiet set of moments in the studio for a short time as all tried to take in what the man had said. The pope looked even more disoriented than before, the Buddhists began chanting in unison with the Dala'i Lama, and the Randers chatted casually among themselves, seemingly unaffected, as several men had already made their moves toward several of the women. Yeshua was smiling, Siddhartha was impassive, and Rand was left to chew her fingernails, as smoking was not allowed in the studio.

Whittle brought the audience back together by saying, "Well folks, that was interesting, but we're just now getting warmed up. Plenty more to come after the commercial break. Next up is some debate time for our three esteemed teachers to directly confront each other's positions and to ..... ."

At that moment, Whittle and everyone in the studio and many outside of it were molecularized in a millisecond as the thunderous roar of a huge explosion from a dirty bomb ripped through the building, leveling it and several adjoining structures. The concussive wave from the massive blast shattered windows in other buildings for a radius of a quarter-mile in all directions. Cars and bodies around the studio were tossed about as if swept aside by a giant invisible hand. The bomb had been planted by Muslim extremists in the basement of the building four days before and had remained undetected by the SWAT team. Over six hundred people inside and outside the building ended their particular sojourn on earth that day.

A little over a mile away in a car waiting at a red light, the man and his companion who had left heard and felt the explosion, the car windows shaking even at that distance from the blast. The man shook his head in disbelief, pounded the dashboard once with his fist, and said, "Just as you predicted."

"Yes," she replied, her eyes glistening with tears. "But what sane person would ever want to be accurate about that?" She leaned back in her seat, her breath choking in her throat. "What a horrible price to pay for the need to be right .... ."

".... And the right to be wrong," the man completed.

Back at the site, in the eerily silent aftermath with smoke billowing and debris still settling to the ground, all that could be heard was high-pitched screaming and the distant wail of many sirens.

Poste

Tears, smiles, and ruminative musings were all part of the woven gestalt as these stories emerged from whatever inner loom artfully produced them. If you cried, laughed, or pondered things in a new way as you read them, you and I in those moments became directly linked in a dance wherein the laws of physics don't apply. And if the ruminative musings in the stories further activated some inner voice in you that aches to be felt, expressed, or heard, a few more words might serve.

As spiritual beings having human experience, we can characterize the narrative of our evolution as a species in many different ways. One way to do this is to view how we have changed our consciousness process as individuals and as a human family over time. Evolving consciousness into new depths, breadths, and heights will always deeply and directly affect how we experience both the context and content of human life, and the values systems that arise in response to those newly explored domains.

In terms of a strictly humanistic sense, prior to the middle of the second millennia in this era of recorded history, the body mainly mediated our experience of human life, moved and driven by primitive emotivity in the form of basic fears related to physical survival, emotive impulses to procreate, to make attachments with each other that later evolved to what we call love, and to create stability in an unpredictable and dangerous world.

In that sense, all of our survival activity and the gradual building of organized civilization were driven by largely body-oriented means and expressions in all areas of life, such as transportation, construction, the growing of food, and the making of clothes and tools by hand.

In those ways the human body was thus generally the basis of our relatedness to life in that segment of our journey human, and was the element of our being, underlain by primitive emotive responses to the challenges of life, experienced as what made us primarily human, whatever we may have believed about ourselves in a religious domain. This era was the childhood of our consciousness evolution, where primitive emotivity moved through body-mediated means, with often savage and inhuman results.

In the middle of the second millennia, the Age of Reason arose, whereby the human mind insinuated itself between primitive emotivity and body-expressions and gradually started to fill the human space, spilling over into many of the activities formerly involving the body, including the body but expanding its possibilities into new realms of ideation and expression.

As the mind began to exert its influence, it also created machines to relieve many of the burdens the body formerly had to carry, making our survival easier, and we then had the time to try and understand the universe in which we found ourselves. When survival thus became more assured with the help of the mind, the possibility of creating experience of human thrival emerged, characterized by states of human meaningfulness and fulfillment.

To create thrival then became a goal of human life, and that led the mind to begin to turn its focus inward to try to understand its own governing dynamics and inner nature. Thus we began to more deeply explore the mind's capacities and extensions and how they contributed to more meaningful and fulfilling human experience, right up to now into our present digital age.

In that drive for meaningfulness and fulfillment, the mind noticed that when primitive unhealthy or immature emotion drove human will, chaos and conflict inevitably followed, which is why mind stepped in to try and assuage those more primitive effects in the first place. In that way, the mind said, 'No, we are not going to let primitive emotional states govern our affairs any longer. We will be more logical in building intentions and actions to create outcomes that need not be so barbarically ragged and destructive.

Human emotion was thus framed as a holdover from less evolved states of mind, and relegated to that which threatened our well-being rather than to be its foundation. Once relegated as such, emotion has been taught to be driven down beneath mind-based consciousness, awaiting the day when it would be redeemed by a different paradigm of human nature. It is exactly that intermediary step of mind designed to outweigh the effects of primitive and chaotic emotion, so necessary while such immature emotion served as the basis for human intentions and actions, that now has hit its own limit.

That mind-based orientation has led to the almost wholly pervasive view in the modern world that a body-based mind is the only real basis for sane and peaceful outcomes of human activity. Virtually all the non-religious areas of human endeavor, including most eastern and modern western spiritualities, maintain this orientation, as well as almost all psychological, scientific, and philosophical arenas of human inquiry. Body-based medicine and physiology are now only reluctantly but surely embracing what seems to be the role of the mind in those domains.

The invitation now is to suggest that just as the mainly child-phase body-oriented dynamisms of our journey began to be replaced by the mind in the middle of the second millennia, which then gradually but inexorably replaced the body as the practical base element of our humanity, here at the beginning of the third millennia, we have come to the limit of the mind-dominated segment of our evolution. That teenage middle era of consciousness evolution of our species has now ended.

No matter how deeply incisive the mind can envision worlds not yet in manifestation and find the means to make them arise, an 'I think, therefore I am' basis of human life, the mind can only envision inner and outer domains such as peace, personal serenity, and spiritual fulfillment, but not create them from the inside out. 'I think, therefore I am' can only create these kinds of experience from the outside in, and must utilize props and accouterments whose artifaction limit the depth of their truer attainment.

This occurs because the mind is inextricably linked to human Will, that which brings what is envisioned by the mind into existence. Will when linked to mind, as the basis of our humanity cannot impart any kind of true or mature inner centeredness, world peace, personal health, serenity, or fulfillment, all the states the lack of which our world suffers so deeply.

We don't suffer from the lack of the latest gadget or technological wonder or from the most effective visualization-state of the mind, we suffer from an inner existential hunger in the heart that neither body nor mind can ever satisfy fully, no matter how deeply they are employed to try to sate that hunger. To address those domains of humanity, in the humanistic sense, we need another paradigm shift equal to the one when teen mind-centered activity began to take over child-phase body-centered human activity.

Now comes the adult phase of our consciousness evolution, characterized by an 'I feel, therefore I am' dynamic. This 'I feel' is not the primitivity of chaos-based or wound-based emotion that mind and so many modern spiritual perspectives eschew. This strata of emotion is not a subset of mind but its foundation and basis, that which the mind is actually a subset of, and so cannot be controlled by it as is so tragically believed and taught by science or mistaken enlightened teachers. Rather, it is the recognition that healthy, mature, and supple human emotion, must finally be seen as the only clean and clear basis to undergird human Will.

In that sense, the human emotional body has always been the foundation of our humanity, the basic currency of human experience and is that from which the mind emanates as the mind can only takes secondary snapshots of human experience. In our earlier evolution, it arose as primitive because that was the only way it could express at that stage.

The state of our current world shows that both the mind-primary orientation in the west and the not-mind primary orientation of human life in the east, has failed utterly. Yet no western empirical mind-based or eastern Buddhistic not-mind-based teacher or teaching will acknowledge this failure. No matter how much mind or not-mind is utilized to solve our human problems, both are able only to treat symptoms and not causes of human suffering, becase suffering is emotive, not mental. Both orientations have believed and taught that either a mind-based or not-mind-based covering over emotivity would allay human suffering. In truth, both pictures only deny that which makes us primarily human, our emotivity, and never address the actual existential infection that causes suffering in the first place.

But when healthy mature emotion starts to drive mind, something we as a species have never known how to actually authentically create until now as the third great era of our species has begun, and as mature emotion drives mind and Will from below, states of far more personal and global peace and serenity finally become manifestable, their arisement previously prevented by a mind-based Will dynamic.

When healthy and supple human emotion thus undergirds mind, Will, and body, individual and global peaceability and mature spiritual embodiment result. This happens because then Love, the most advanced and basic emotion of all, is finally able to drive Will and mind from beneath, something our Creator has been waiting a very long time for us to finally realize.

The ability to mature the human emotional body, which no form of psychological therapy or religio-spiritual process has ever been able to create because of their mystical-, mind-, and body-based paradigms of human behaviors, is the holy grail so long veiled by our fledgling state of consciousness as a species. Its emergence into all of our inner and outer worlds will change even more about our human experience than the shift that occurred when mind took over from body, because it will gradually and substantively illuminate what we have missed as to how humanity and divinity have never been different from each other, splayed only by our teenage modes of consciousness until now.

As such, we as a species have been moving from outer to inner in discovering our true nature as spiritual beings having human experience. It is now time to recognize that feeling and emotion is what makes us most human, and not mind-processes or body physiology. Emotion has always been primary to mind and body, and is the most basic expression of Spirit as It breathes through our humanity. Making the movement from mind- and body-based paradigms to emotive-based ones that in themselves incorporate Spirit, changes the very heart of all the messages of the great spiritual teachers, redefining what they have taught and allowing new destinations never imagined by those teachers, mired as they were in earlier phases of our evolution of consciousness.

In that way, all the great teachers from the Axial Age began the quest to define and attain the spiritual context for our human lives. But those could only be introductions to that quest. Embodiment of most of what those teachers offered in a bygone age awaited the moment until humankind evolved enough to realize that mature emotion is the basis for both our humanness and spiritualness and their intrinsic linkage, and not just a realm of some kind of residue left over from more primitive instincts and impulses.

Embodying the truth that we are emotive beings first, mental being second, and physical beings third is the only humanistic basis for spiritual exploration that does not splay the divine from the human: the split of our humanity and our divinity taught and thus experienced by all religions and spiritual teachings east and west is wholly an artifact of misdiagnosing our human nature as primarily mental (mind) or physical (body).

Once emotion finds the way to alchemically transmute from the iron of its instinctual immature forms, the gold of mature emotion becomes the foundation for true spiritual maturity beyond states of mere spiritual attainment, and the means to finally embody the divinity of which the former teachers from earlier, less evolved eras spoke.

So if these stories inspire you to discover for yourself what view of life allows access to identify, heal, and embody that which the characters in these stories experience, your individual version of the human narrative is invited to look further into the paradigm of Theohumanity, which teaches the triple embodiment of Personhood, Sagehood, and Sainthood consciousnesses, and with that, access to the state of Enheartenment beyond enlightenment, that which has always been both the legacy and final destination of our species' journey in spirit as flesh.

Photo©Bryon DeVore

"........it is now that time in history for both western revelatory-based and eastern ego transcendence-based spiritual systems to realize that their time in our evolution of consciousness is over, as both demonize the self's journey through flesh-expression in profound and limiting ways. It is now time for a humanistic-based spirituality that teaches us how to live into our humanity as divine in itself within new paradigmatic guidelines of self-discovery whose authority lies within the human heart and not without."

Daniel Barron

Biography

After his Nondual awakening in the tradition of Zen Buddhism in the 1980's, Daniel Barron realized almost all distortions and misunderstandings in psychological and spiritual teachings involved how neither ego-based nor non-ego-based paths that address the cause of suffering adequately understand the true nature and significance of the human emotional body.

As a result, Barron created an overall paradigm and personal practice for the enlightenment of the human emotional body called Emotional Body Enlightenment (EBE) that challenges 100 years of psychological premise and practice, and a new psychospiritual paradigm called Theohumanity that challenges 5000 years of eastern transcendental teaching about the criteria for attaining enlightenment, western models of what we call God, and the nature of what we call Universal Oneness and Love.

Barron is founder of Project Theohumanity, and author of *Enheartenment*, *There's no Such thing as a negative Emotion*, *Him*, *Gnospel*, and a theatrical play, *Josie*. Barron offers weeklong retreats, weekend seminars, and personal sessions.

Upcoming works by DS Barron

Doorway of the Dance   2011

A new paradigm of human relationality that redefines the nature and transaction elements of both shadow-based codependency and healthy interdependency in all domains of relational space

the Blood in the Bread   2011

How the safety and security we immaturely project into and expect from money creates personal and global financial dystrophy and keeps us mired in ongoing states of arrested emotional development

Frozen Feminine-Muddled Masculine   2011

Challenging millennia of personal, cultural, religious, and spiritual distortion of male-female transaction dynamics

Moonlight in the Mist   2011

A scathing metaphysical critique of the bankruptcy of Buddhism and transcendence of selfhood that redefines the meaning and context of enightened access to the Nondual Aspect of Divine Being

Lantern to the Light   2011

How all pre-egoic based religions and spiritualities of the east and west marginalize the self and forever distort access to the Maker Creator Aspect of Divine Being

For more information and ordering please visit
www.theohumanity.org
or email info@theohumanity.org